**"They're coming!"** a woman shrieked, and instantly everyone was turning and pushing in order to get away.

They must have bolted as blindly as a flock of sheep. The crowd jammed up where the road gets narrow between the high banks, and a desperate struggle occurred. Not all of the crowd escaped; three people, two women and a little boy, were crushed and trampled and left to die in the terror and darkness.

## A Background Note about
*The War of the Worlds*

*The War of the Worlds* was published in 1898, a time when very few facts were known about Mars. Astronomers were just beginning to seriously study the planet, and news stories about their observations were generating great interest. In creating *The War of the Worlds*, H.G. Wells was able to capitalize on the public's curiosity about the red planet and what—or who—might exist there.

# H.G. WELLS

# THE WAR OF THE WORLDS

Edited by Denton Cairnes
Afterword by Beth Johnson

 THE TOWNSEND LIBRARY

# THE WAR OF THE WORLDS

**TP**  **THE TOWNSEND LIBRARY**

For more titles in the Townsend Library,
visit our website: www.townsendpress.com

ISBN 13: 978-1-59194-075-3
ISBN 10: 1-59194-075-3

Library of Congress Control Number:
2006933646

# Contents

## BOOK TWO
### The Earth Under the Martians

## AFTERWORD

# BOOK ONE

# THE
# COMING
# OF
# THE
# MARTIANS

**CHAPTER 1**

# The Eve of the War

**IN** the last years of the nineteenth century, no one believed that our world was being watched by alien beings with intelligence greater than man's. And even if we knew of the alien's superior intelligence, no one would have believed that they were as mortal as man. As men busied themselves with their various concerns, they were being watched and studied, perhaps almost like a man with a microscope might study the tiny creatures that swarm in a drop of water.

No one gave a thought to the older worlds of space as sources of human danger, or thought that these worlds might contain life. Yet across the gulf of space, alien minds that are to our minds as ours are to those of the savage beasts—intellects vast and unsympathetic—regarded our Earth with envious eyes, and slowly and surely drew up their plans against us. And early in the twentieth century came the great invasion.

The planet Mars, if I may remind the reader,

revolves about the sun at a distance of 140,000,000 miles, and the light and heat it receives from the sun are barely half of the amount received by our world. It is older than Earth, and life on its surface must have begun long before life started on Earth.

The cooling that will someday occur on our planet has already started on this neighboring planet. Its physical condition is largely a mystery, but we know that even in its equatorial region the midday temperature barely approaches that of our coldest winter. Its atmosphere is more diluted than ours, its oceans have almost disappeared, and as its seasons change, huge snowcaps gather and melt at both its north and south poles and occasionally expand to cover its temperate zones.

The last stage of existence, which for our world is still incredibly far in the future, has become a present day situation for the inhabitants of Mars. Their immediate problem of survival has brightened their intellects, enlarged their powers, and hardened their hearts. And as they look across space with instruments and intelligence such as we have scarcely dreamed of, they see, only 35,000,000 miles away, a morning star of hope. They see our warmer planet, green with vegetation and blue with water. They see a world bursting with fertility, with glimpses through its drifting clouds of broad stretches of populous country, green farms and forests, and deep blue seas.

And we men, the dominant creatures who inhabit this Earth, must be to them at least as alien and lowly as the monkeys and apes are to us. The intellectual side of man already admits that life is a struggle for existence, and it would seem that this is also the belief on Mars. Their world is at its last stage, and our world is still crowded with life, but crowded only with what they regard as inferior animals. To carry warfare to us is their only escape from the destruction that, generation after generation, is creeping over them.

Before we judge them too harshly, we must remember what ruthless and utter destruction our own species has brought to its fellow human beings as well as any animal species that got in its way. Can we complain if the Martians make war in the same spirit?

The Martians seem to have carried out their preparations with almost perfect precision. Had our primitive telescopes and other instruments permitted it, we might have seen the gathering trouble. Men have studied the red planet for the last hundred years but failed to correctly interpret the changes that they documented so well. All that time, the Martians must have been getting ready.

As our two planets came close to each other a few years ago, a bright light was seen on Mars by several astronomical observatories. We know now that this light occurred as they manufactured a huge gun barrel. They positioned the gun in a large pit and used it to fire immense projectiles, crammed full of equipment, machines, and Martian warriors, at our planet.

The invasion storm rained down on us just a short time later. Astronomers exchanged exciting news about a huge outbreak of flaming gas from the red planet. Examination by spectroscope indicated a mass of gas, mainly hydrogen, moving with enormous speed toward Earth. This jet of fire disappeared almost immediately. One scientist compared it to a colossal puff of flame suddenly and violently squirted out "like flaming gases blasting out of a gun."

It proved to be an appropriate phrase. Yet the next day there was little in the papers, and the world went on in ignorance of the gravest danger that ever threatened the human race. I might not have heard of the eruption at all had I not bumped into a well-known astronomer at my university. He was immensely excited at the news, and invited me up to his observatory for a look at the red planet.

In spite of all that has happened since, I still remember that vigil very distinctly: the black and silent observatory, the shadowed lantern throwing a feeble glow on the floor in the corner, the little slit in the roof with the starlight twinkling above. Looking through the telescope, one saw a circle of deep black and the little red planet floating in the center. It seemed like such a little thing, so bright and small and still.

Invisible to us because it was so remote, flying swiftly and steadily toward us across that incredible distance, drawing nearer every minute by so many thousands of miles, came the thing they were sending us. That thing, and the others that followed, would soon bring incredible struggle and calamity and death to Earth. I never dreamed of it then as I watched; no one on Earth dreamed of that unerring missile.

That night, too, there was another jet of gas streaming out from the distant planet. I saw it. It was a reddish flash—the slightest projection out from the planet's surface. I called my friend to look, and then listened while he excitedly described the explosion of gas that came out toward us.

That night another invisible missile started on its way to the Earth, just twenty-four hours after the first one. I remember how I stood there, little suspecting the meaning of what I had seen and all that it would soon bring to me. We watched until one o'clock, and then gave up and walked toward his house. Down below in the darkness was the peaceful village where we lived and its hundreds of people, sleeping in peace.

That night my friend was full of speculation

about Mars but scoffed at my idea that its inhabitants were signaling us. His idea was that meteorites might be falling on the distant planet, or that a huge volcanic explosion was in progress. He pointed out how unlikely it was that organic evolution had taken the same direction in the two different planets.

"The chances against anything manlike on Mars are a million to one," he said.

Hundreds of observers saw the puff of flame that night and the night after, and again the night after; and so on for ten nights, a flame each night. Why the eruptions stopped after the tenth, no one has attempted to explain. Dense clouds of smoke, visible through a powerful telescope on Earth as little gray, fluctuating patches, spread through the clearness of the red planet's atmosphere and obscured its more familiar features.

Even the daily papers woke up to the disturbances at last, and stories appeared here, there, and everywhere concerning the volcanoes on Mars. And, unsuspected, those missiles the Martians had fired at us came closer, rushing many miles a second through the empty gulf of space, hour by hour and day by day, nearer and nearer.

It seems incredible to me now that men could continue with their petty concerns while that fate was hanging over us. For my own part, I was busy writing a series of philosophical papers

discussing the development of moral ideas as civilization progressed.

One night (the first missile was probably only
10,000,000 miles away) I went for a walk with
my wife. It was a cloudless night with bright
starlight, and I explained the Signs of the Zodiac
to her, and pointed out Mars, a bright dot of red
light just above the horizon. There were lights in
the upper windows of the houses as the people
went to bed. From the railway station in the distance came the sounds of trains, ringing and
rumbling, softened almost into melody by the
distance. My wife pointed out the brightness of
the red, green, and yellow signal lights hanging
in a framework against the sky. It seemed so safe
and tranquil.

**CHAPTER 2**

# The Falling Star

**THEN** came the night of the first falling star. It was seen early in the morning, rushing toward the east, a line of flame high in the atmosphere. Hundreds must have seen it, and taken it for an ordinary falling star. Many witnesses said it had a greenish streak trailing behind that glowed for a few seconds.

I was at home at that hour writing in my study and although my windows face east, I did not see anything. Yet this strangest of all things that ever came to Earth from outer space must have fallen while I was sitting there. Some of those who saw its flight say it traveled with a hissing sound. I myself heard nothing. Many people in the surrounding villages must have seen it fall and thought that it was only another meteorite. No one went out to look for the fallen star that night.

But very early the next morning, my friend the astronomer, who lived nearby, got up to go out and look for it. He had seen the shooting star the previous night and thought that it landed somewhere toward the east only a few miles away. He found it soon after dawn not far from our local sand pits. An enormous hole had been made by the impact of the projectile, and the sand and gravel had been thrown out in every direction, forming heaps visible a mile and a half away. Some of the surrounding grass was on fire, and a thin wisp of smoke rose against the dawn.

The thing itself lay almost entirely buried in sand. The uncovered part had the appearance of a huge cylinder, its outline softened by a thick coating of mud. It was about thirty feet in diameter. He approached it, surprised at the size and more so at the shape, since most meteorites are rounded, porous rocks. It was still too hot from its flight through the air for him to get close. He heard a noise inside the cylinder but thought that the cooling of its surface might be the cause. At that time, it had not occurred to him that it might be hollow.

He remained standing at the edge of the pit, staring at the thing, astonished by its unusual shape. It dawned on him that some intelligent beings had made the thing. The early morning was wonderfully still, and the sun, just clearing the pine trees, was already warm. He did not remember hearing any birds that morning, there was no breeze stirring, and the only sounds were the faint movements from inside the cylinder. He was completely alone out in the fields.

Then suddenly, he noticed that some of the mud that covered the thing was falling off the circular edge of the end. It was dropping off in flakes. A large piece suddenly came off and fell with a loud noise that frightened him.

For a minute he did not realize what this meant, and, although the heat was excessive, he slid down into the pit to see the thing more clearly. He was still thinking that the cooling of the body was causing the noise, but then saw that the mud was falling only from the end of the cylinder.

And then he observed that the circular top of the cylinder was rotating very slowly. It was such a gradual movement that he discovered it only by observing that a black mark that had been near him five minutes ago was now on the other side. Even then he did not understand what this meant until he heard a muffled grating sound and saw the black mark move an inch or so. Then he realized that the cylinder was artificial—hollow—with an end that screwed out. Something inside the cylinder was unscrewing the top.

"Good heavens!" he thought. "There's a man in it—men in it. Half roasted to death. Trying to escape!"

At once, with a quick mental leap, he linked the cylinder with the flash on Mars. The thought of the confined creature was so dreadful to him that he forgot the heat and went forward to the cylinder to help turn the lid. But luckily, the heat stopped him before he could burn his hands on the still-glowing metal. He stood there for a moment, then turned, scrambled out of the pit, and went off running toward the village.

The time then must have been somewhere about six o'clock in the morning. He met a man driving a wagon and tried to make him understand, but the tale he told and his appearance were so wild, that the man simply drove on. He was equally unsuccessful with the owner of the grocery store who was just unlocking the doors of his shop. He calmed down a little and when he saw a neighbor he knew, a respected London journalist, he made himself understood.

"Hey there!" he called, "did you see that shooting star last night?"

"Yes, what about it?"

"It's out in the fields about two miles east of here!"

"Good Lord! A fallen meteorite! That'll make a good story."

"But it's something more than a meteorite. It's a cylinder—an artificial cylinder, man! And there's something inside!"

The journalist stood up and said, "What's that? What did you say?"

My friend told him all that he had seen. The journalist stood there for a minute or so taking it in and then snatched up his jacket and came out into the road. The two men hurried back to the crash site, and found the cylinder still lying in the same position. But now the sounds inside had stopped, and a thin circle of bright metal was showing between the top and the body of the cylinder. Air was either entering or escaping at the rim with a slight sizzling sound.

They listened, rapped on the burnt metal with a stick, and, getting no response, they both concluded that the man or men inside must be dead.

Of course, the two were unable to do anything to remove the lid. They went off back to town again to get help. One can imagine them, covered with sand, excited and disordered, running up the little street in the bright sunlight just as the shop folks were taking down their shutters and people were opening their bedroom windows. The journalist went into the railway station to telegraph the news to London. The previous newspaper articles had somewhat prepared people for the idea of something falling to Earth.

By eight o'clock, a number of boys and unemployed men had already left for the site to see the "dead men from Mars." That was the form the story took. I heard it first from my newspaper boy about a quarter to nine when I went out to get my paper. I was naturally startled, and lost no time in going out to the sand pits.

# CHAPTER 3

# At the Sand Pit

I found more that twenty people milling around and looking down at the cylinder in its huge hole. Among these were a couple of cyclists, a gardener I occasionally employed, a girl carrying a baby, the butcher and his little boy, and two or three loafers and golf caddies who usually hung around the railway station. There was very little talking. Most of them were staring quietly at the end of the cylinder. I imagine the lack of charred corpses was somewhat disappointing to these folks. I looked down into the pit and thought I felt a faint vibration under my feet.

I walked around the edge of the pit, and it was only when I got close to the thing that the strangeness of the object really hit me. At first glance, it was no more exciting than an overturned carriage or a tree blown across the road. It looked like a rusty water tank. It required a certain amount of scientific education to see that the yellowish-white metal that gleamed in the crack between the lid and the body of the cylinder had an unfamiliar color. "Extra-terrestrial" had no meaning for most of the onlookers.

At that time I knew that the thing had come from the planet Mars, but I did not think that it could contain any living creature. I thought the unscrewing might be automatic, although I still believed that there were men on Mars. My mind latched onto the idea of the thing containing some kind of manuscript and on the difficulties in translation that might arise. I wondered whether we would find objects of scientific value in it, and so forth. Yet I could see it was a little large to contain these types of items. I felt an impatience to see it opened. Around eleven, since nothing seemed to be happening, I walked back to my home, full of such thoughts. Once there, I found it difficult to get to work on my research.

By the afternoon the appearance of things being normal had changed very much. The early editions of the evening papers had startled London with enormous headlines:

"A MESSAGE RECEIVED FROM MARS."
"REMARKABLE STORY THREE MILES SOUTH OF THE CITY," and so forth.

I went back to the sand pits to check things out. There were half a dozen horse-drawn cabs from the rail station standing in the road and a couple of fancy carriages. Besides that, there was quite a heap of bicycles. In addition, a large number of people must have walked from the surrounding towns, so that there was a considerable crowd.

It was glaringly hot, not a cloud in the sky or a breath of wind, and the only shadow was that of the few scattered pine trees. The burning grass had been extinguished, but the level ground to the west was blackened as far as one could see, and still giving off streamers of smoke.

Going to the edge of the pit, I looked down and found a group of about half a dozen men—my friend the astronomer, and a tall, fair-haired man that I afterward learned was Professor Stent, the Royal Astronomer, with several workmen using spades and pickaxes. Stent was giving directions in a clear, high-pitched voice.

A large portion of the cylinder had been uncovered, though its lower end was still embedded in the sand. As soon as my friend saw me among the crowd on the edge of the pit, he called to me to come down. After a quick introduction, Stent asked me if I would mind going over to the local police station.

The growing crowd, he said, was becoming a serious impediment to their excavations, especially the boys. He wanted a light railing put up, and a police officer to help keep the people back. He told me that a faint stirring was occasionally audible inside the cylinder, but that the workmen had failed to unscrew the top. The case appeared to be enormously thick, and it was possible that the faint sounds we heard represented a living being inside.

I was glad to do as he asked, and after running my errand, it was a little past five, so I went home, had some tea, and talked with my wife about all the excitement.

### CHAPTER 4

# The Cylinder Opens

**WHEN** I returned to the site the sun was setting. The crowd around the pit had increased, and stood out black against the lemon yellow of the sky—a couple of hundred people, perhaps. There were raised voices, and some sort of struggle appeared to be going on. As I drew nearer I heard Stent's voice: "Keep back! Keep back!"

A boy came running toward me shouting, "It's a-movin' and a-screwin' out! I don't like it. I'm a-goin' 'ome, I am!"

I went into the crowd. There were maybe two or three hundred people elbowing and jostling one another, the few ladies present being by no means the least active.

"He's fallen in the pit!" cried someone.

"Keep back!" said several.

The crowd swayed a little, and I elbowed my way through. Everyone seemed greatly excited. I heard a peculiar humming sound from the pit.

"I say!" yelled my friend when he saw me,

"help keep these idiots back. We don't know what's in the confounded thing, you know!"

I saw a young man standing on the cylinder and trying to scramble out of the hole. The crowd had pushed him in.

The end of the cylinder was being screwed out from inside. Nearly two feet of shining screw threads were visible. Somebody bumped against me, and I narrowly missed falling into the pit. I turned away, and as I did so the screw must have come out, for the lid of the cylinder fell on the ground with a ringing sound. I stuck my elbow into the person behind me, and turned my head toward the thing again. For a moment that circular cavity seemed perfectly black. I had the sunset in my eyes.

I think everyone expected to see a man emerge—possibly something a little unlike us terrestrial men, but in all essentials a man. I know I did. But, looking, I eventually saw something stirring within the shadow: grayish billowy movements, one above another, and then two luminous disks—like eyes. Then something resembling a little gray snake, about the thickness of a walking stick, coiled up out of the writhing mass, and wriggled in the air toward me—and then another snake followed behind.

A sudden chill came over me. There was a loud shriek from a woman behind. I half turned, keeping my eyes fixed on the cylinder, from which other tentacles were now emerging, and began pushing my way back from the edge of the pit. I saw astonishment changing to horror on the faces of the people around me. There was a general movement backward along with an increase in the noise of the crowd. I saw the young man still struggling and trying to get out of the pit. I found myself alone, and saw the people on the other side of the pit running off, Stent among them. I looked again at the cylinder, and unspeakable terror gripped me. I stood petrified and staring.

A big grayish rounded bulk, the size, perhaps, of a bear, was rising slowly out of the cylinder. As it bulged up and caught the light, it glistened like wet leather.

Two large dark-colored eyes were focused on me. The mass that framed them, apparently the head of the thing, was rounded, and had, one might say, a face. Under the eyes there was a mouth that quivered and panted, and dripped saliva. The whole creature heaved and pulsated convulsively. A tentacle-like appendage gripped the edge of the cylinder, another swayed in the air.

Those who have never seen a living Martian can not imagine the strange horror of its appearance. The peculiar V-shaped mouth with its pointed upper lip, the absence of brow ridges, the absence of a chin beneath the wedge-like lower lip, the incessant quivering of its mouth, the groups of tentacles, the tumultuous breathing of the lungs in a strange atmosphere, the evident heaviness and painfulness of movement due to the greater gravitational pull of the Earth—above all, the extraordinary intensity of the immense eyes—were at once vital, inhuman, crippled and monstrous. There was something like a fungus appearance to the oily brown skin, something in the clumsy deliberation of the tedious movements that was unspeakably nasty. Even at this first encounter, this first glimpse, I was overcome with disgust and dread.

Suddenly the monster toppled over the brim of the cylinder and fell into the pit with a thud like a great mass of leather falling on the floor. I heard it give a peculiar thick cry, and immediately, another of these creatures appeared in the deep shadow of the opening.

I turned and, running madly, made for the first group of trees, perhaps a hundred yards away; but I ran sideways and stumbling, because I could not turn my face away from these things.

I stopped when I reached the trees, panting, and awaited further developments. The fields around the sand pits were dotted with people, standing like myself in a half-fascinated terror, staring at these creatures, or rather at the heaped gravel at the edge of the pit in which they lay. And then, with a renewed horror, I saw a round, black object bobbing up and down on the edge of the pit. It was the head of the young man who had fallen in, but looking like a little black ball against the hot western sun. Now he got his shoulder and knee up, and again he seemed to slip back until only his head was visible. Suddenly he vanished, and I imagined a faint shriek. I had a momentary impulse to go back and help him that my fears overruled.

I looked over and saw that everything was hidden in the deep pit and by the heaps of sand caused by the impact of the cylinder. Anyone coming along the road would have been amazed at the sight—a dwindling crowd of perhaps a hundred people standing in a great irregular circle, in ditches, behind bushes, behind gates and hedges, saying little to one another and staring, staring hard at a few heaps of sand. At the edge of the sand pits was a row of abandoned vehicles with their horses feeding out of nosebags or pawing the ground.

CHAPTER 5

# The Heat Ray

**AFTER** the glimpse I had had of the Martians emerging from their cylinder, a kind of fascination paralyzed my actions. I remained standing knee-deep in the grass, staring at the mound that hid them. I was a battleground of fear and curiosity.

I did not dare to go back toward the pit, but I felt a passionate longing to peer into it. I began walking in a big curve, seeking some vantage point and continually looking at the sand heaps that hid these newcomers to our Earth. Once, a leash of thin black whips, like the arms of an octopus, flashed across the sunset and was immediately withdrawn, and afterward a thin rod rose up, joint by joint, topped by a circular disk that spun with a wobbling motion. What could be going on there?

Most of the spectators had gathered in one or two groups—one a little crowd on my right, the other a knot of people over on my left. Evidently, they shared my mental conflict. There were few near me. I approached one man—a neighbor of mine, though I did not know his name—but it was hardly a time for articulate conversation.

"What ugly brutes!" he panted. "Good God! What ugly brutes!" He repeated this over and over again.

"Did you see a man in the pit?" I asked; but he did not answer.

The sunset faded to twilight before anything further happened. The crowd on the left seemed to grow. The other little knots of people dispersed. There was no sign of movement from the pit.

It was this, as much as anything, that gave people courage, and I suppose the new arrivals also helped to restore confidence. At any rate, as dusk fell, a slow, intermittent movement began, a movement that seemed to gather force as the stillness of the evening around the cylinder remained unbroken. Vertical black figures in twos and threes would advance, stop, watch, and advance again, spreading out as they did so in a thin irregular crescent that promised to encircle the pit. I, too, began to move toward the pit.

Then I saw that some men had walked boldly into the sand pits. Almost immediately I heard the clatter of hoofs and the grinding of wheels as the cab drivers quickly drove their rigs away. After this, I noted a little knot of men approaching the pit—the man in front was waving a white flag.

This appeared to be some kind of deputation to communicate with the Martians. Apparently there had been a hasty consultation, and since the Martians were evidently, in spite of their repulsive forms, intelligent creatures, it had been decided to show them, by approaching them with signals, that we too were intelligent.

Flutter, flutter, went the flag, first to the right, then to the left. It was too far for me to recognize anyone, but afterward I learned that my friend and Stent were with some others in this attempt at communication. A number of other dim figures followed the group with the flag at a discreet distance.

Suddenly there was a flash of light, and some luminous, greenish smoke came out of the pit in three distinct puffs. The light beams pointed straight up, one after the other, straight into the still air followed by the smoke. At the same time a faint hissing sound was heard.

Next to the pit stood the little wedge of people with the white flag, a little stationary knot of small vertical dark shapes on the black ground. As the green smoke arose, their faces flashed out pallid green, and faded again as it vanished. Then slowly, the hissing passed into a humming, into a long, loud, droning noise. Slowly a humped shape rose out of the pit, and a beam of light seemed to flicker out of it toward the group of people.

Suddenly, flashes of actual flame, leaping from one to another, sprang from the scattered group of men. It was as if they were doused with gasoline that then flashed into white flame. It was as if each man were suddenly and momentarily turned to fire. I then saw them, by the light of their own destruction, running, staggering and falling, and their supporters turning to flee.

I stood staring, not yet realizing that this was death leaping from man to man in that little distant crowd. All I felt was that it was something very strange. An almost noiseless and blinding flash of light, and a man burst into flames, fell on the ground and lay still! As the shaft of light and the unseen beam of heat passed over them, pine trees exploded into fire, and every dry bush in its path burst into a mass of flames. And far away at the edge of the field, I saw trees and hedges and wooden buildings suddenly set on fire.

It was sweeping around steadily, this flaming death, this invisible, inevitable sword of heat. I saw it coming toward me by the flashing bushes it touched, and was too astounded to stir from my spot. I heard the crackle of fire in the sand pits and the sudden squeal of a horse. Then it was as if an invisible yet intensely heated finger were drawn between me and the Martians, and all along a curving line beyond the sand pits the dark ground smoked and crackled. Something fell with a crash far away to the left, and then the hissing and humming ceased, and the black, domelike object sank slowly out of sight into the pit.

All this had happened with such swiftness that I had stood motionless, dumbfounded and dazzled by the flashes of light. Had that death swept through a full circle, it would have killed me as I stood there in shock. But it passed by and spared me, and left the night around me suddenly dark and unfamiliar.

The pit and fields around it now seemed dark almost to blackness, except where the roadways lay gray and pale under the deep blue sky of the early night. It was dark, and suddenly devoid of men. Overhead the stars were coming out, and in the west the sky was still a pale, bright, almost greenish blue. The tops of the pine trees and the roofs of the nearby town appeared sharp and black against the western afterglow. The Martians and their mysterious weapons were completely invisible, except for that thin mast holding up their constantly moving mirror. Patches of bush and isolated trees here and there still smoked and glowed, and the houses touched by the heat beam were sending up spires of flame into the stillness of the evening air.

Nothing was changed except for that and a terrible astonishment. The little group of black specks with the flag of white had been swept out of existence, and the stillness of the evening, so it seemed to me, had scarcely been broken.

I realized that I was out here alone, helpless, and unprotected. Suddenly, like something falling on me from above, came—fear. With an effort, I turned and began a stumbling run through the grass.

The fear I felt was no rational fear, but a panic terror not only of the Martians, but of the dusk and stillness all around me. It had such an extraordinary effect in unmanning me that I felt myself running and weeping silently like a child. Once I had turned away, I did not dare to look back.

I remember I felt like I was being played with, and that soon, when I was almost safe, this mysterious death—as swift as the passage of light—would leap up from the pit and strike me down.

It still amazes me how the Martians could kill men so swiftly and silently. They were able to generate intense heat and project it in a beam against any object they chose by means of a polished parabolic mirror. It was explained in the papers as similar to how the parabolic mirror of a lighthouse projects a beam of light. But no one has figured out the details of how it was done. When it strikes, whatever is combustible explodes into flame, lead runs like water, it softens iron, cracks and melts glass, and when it hits water, the water bursts into steam.

That night, around the pit, nearly forty people lay on the ground under the starlight. They were charred and distorted beyond recognition, and all night long the surrounding fields were deserted and brightly ablaze.

Previously, Stent and the others, anticipating the possibility of some conflict, had gone to town and telegraphed for the help of the army to protect these strange creatures from violence. After that, they returned to lead that ill-fated deputation. The description of their death, as it was seen by the crowd, tallies very closely with my own impressions: the three puffs of green smoke, the deep humming sound, and the flashes of flame.

But that crowd of people had a far narrower escape than mine. Only the fact that a mound of sand intercepted the lower part of the Heat Ray saved them. Had the elevation of the parabolic mirror been a few yards higher, no one would have lived to tell the tale. They saw the flashes, and the men falling, and an invisible hand, as it were, lit the bushes as it moved toward them through the twilight. Then, with a whistling note that rose above the droning of the pit, the beam swung over their heads, lighting the tops of the trees that line the road, and setting alight the house nearest the corner.

In the sudden thud, hiss, and glare of the igniting trees, the panic-stricken crowd seemed to have swayed and hesitated for a moment. Sparks and burning twigs began to fall into the road, and single leaves floated around like puffs of flame. Hats and dresses caught fire. There were shrieks and shouts, and suddenly a mounted policeman came galloping through the confusion with his hands clasped over his head, screaming at the top of his lungs.

"They're coming!" a woman shrieked, and instantly everyone was turning and pushing in order to get away. They must have bolted as blindly as a flock of sheep. The crowd jammed up where the road gets narrow between the high banks, and a desperate struggle occurred. Not all of the crowd escaped; three people, two women and a little boy, were crushed and trampled and left to die in the terror and darkness.

# CHAPTER 6

# How I Reached Home

**FOR** my own part, I don't remember anything about my flight except blundering against trees and stumbling through the grass. It seemed like the invisible terrors of the Martians were all around me; that pitiless sword of heat seemed whirling to and fro, flourishing overhead where it might descend and smite the life out of me. I came to the road and ran as fast as I could.

At last I could go no farther. I was exhausted, as I staggered and fell by the wayside. I was near the bridge that crosses the canal by the gasworks. I fell and lay still. I finally sat up, and for a moment could not understand how I got here. My terror had fallen from me like a garment. A few minutes before, there had only been three real things in my mind—the immensity of the night and space and nature, my own feebleness and anguish, and the near approach of death. Now it was as if my point of view changed abruptly. I was myself again—a decent, ordinary citizen. The silent fields, the impulse of my flight, the terrifying flames, seemed like a dream. I asked myself if these things had really happened. I could not believe it.

I got up and started over the bridge. My mind was a blank wonder. My muscles and nerves seemed drained of their strength. I staggered like a drunk. A workman carrying a basket came into view from the other direction. Beside him ran a little boy. He passed me, wishing me good night. I answered his greeting with a meaningless mumble and went on over the bridge.

I saw a train in the distance, a billowing tumult of white, fire-lit smoke, and a long caterpillar of lighted windows went flying south—clatter, clatter, clap, rap, and it was gone. A dim group of people talked in front of one of the houses at the edge of town. It was all so real and so familiar. And then I thought of that obscenity behind me! Such things, I told myself, could not be.

Perhaps I am a man of exceptional moods. At times I suffer from the strangest sense of detachment from the world around me; I seem to watch it all from the outside, from somewhere inconceivably remote, out of time, out of space, out of the stress and tragedy of it all. This feeling was very strong with me that night.

I could not reconcile this picture of serenity I was approaching with the swift death striking out not two miles away. There was a noise of machinery from the gasworks, and the electric lamps were all alight. I stopped at the group of people.

"Any news from the sand pits?" I asked.

"What's that?" said one of the men, turning.

"What news from the sand pits?" I said.

"Ain't you just *been* there?" asked the men.

"People seem fair silly about that place," said a woman behind the men. "What's it all about?"

"Haven't you heard about the men from Mars? The creatures from Mars?"

"I've heard quite enough, thank you very much!" said the woman, and all three of them laughed.

I felt foolish and angry. I tried and found I could not tell them what I had seen. They laughed again at my broken sentences.

"You'll hear more real soon," I said, and went on to my home.

I startled my wife, waiting at the doorway, with my haggard appearance. I went into the dining room, sat down, drank some wine, and, after I got myself together, told her the things I had seen.

"There is one thing in our favor," I said in a vain attempt to keep her calm; "they are the most sluggish things I ever saw crawl. They may stay in the pit and kill people who come near them, but they cannot get out! My God, they were horrid looking beasts!"

"Don't, dear!" said my wife, knitting her brows and putting her hand on mine, trying to calm me down. My wife, at least, did not find my experience unbelievable. When I saw how deadly pale her face was, I abruptly stopped talking.

"They may come here," she said again and again.

I tried to get her to take some wine, and attempted to reassure her.

"They can barely move," I said.

I began to comfort her and myself by repeating the impossibility of the Martians establishing themselves on Earth. In particular, I stressed the gravitational difficulty. On Earth, the force of gravity is three times what it is on the surface of Mars. A Martian would feel like he weighed three times more than on Mars, but his muscular strength would be the same. Both the newspapers I read the next morning restated this concept, but both overlooked, just as I did, two obvious modifying influences.

The atmosphere on Earth contains far more oxygen than does the atmosphere on Mars. We now know the invigorating influences of this excess of oxygen on the Martians did much to counterbalance the increased weight of their bodies. We also overlooked the fact that the Martian's engineering and mechanical intelligence was able to reduce their need for muscular exertion.

But I did not consider these points at the time, and so my reasoning was against the chances of the invaders. With wine and food, the confidence of my own table, and the necessity of reassuring my wife, I grew courageous and secure.

"They have done a foolish thing," said I, fingering my wineglass. "They are dangerous because, no doubt, they are mad with terror. Perhaps they expected to find no living things— certainly no intelligent living things. An artillery shell fired into the pit will kill them all."

At the end of our meal, I sat thinking about the events of the day, regretting the crowd's rashness, and denouncing the shortsightedness of the timid, weak Martians. I did not know it, but that was the last civilized dinner I was to eat for many strange and terrible days.

# CHAPTER 7

# Friday Night

**THE** most extraordinary thing, of all the strange happenings that day, was the dovetailing of the commonplace habits of our social order with the first events that were to topple that social order. Many people had heard of the cylinder, of course, and talked about it with interest, but did not realize how important an event they were discussing.

In our immediate area, the great majority of people were calm. I have already described the behavior of the men and women to whom I spoke. All over the district, people were dining; working men were relaxing after the labors of the day; children were being put to bed; young couples were wandering through the lanes holding hands; and students sat over their books.

Maybe there was a murmur in the village streets, a new and dominant topic in the bars and restaurants, and here and there an eyewitness of the occurrences. But for the most part, the daily routine of working, eating, drinking, and sleeping went on as it had for countless years—as though no planet Mars existed in the sky.

At the railway station, trains were stopping and going, passengers were getting off and waiting, and everything was proceeding in the most ordinary way. A boy from town was selling papers with that afternoon's news. People traveling toward London looked into the darkness outside their carriage windows and saw only an occasional flickering, flaming, spark dance up from the direction of the pits and the nearby village. That, and a red glow, and a thin veil of smoke drifting across the stars, would have made them think that nothing more serious than a trash fire was burning. It was only around the edge of the sand pits that any disturbance was perceptible. It was there where they would have seen half a dozen houses burning on the town's border.

A curious crowd lingered restlessly, some people were coming and going but the crowd remained. I learned later that one or two adventurous souls went into the darkness and crawled near the Martians; but they never returned. Every once in a while a spotlight, like the beam of a warship's searchlight, swept the fields, and the Heat Ray was ready to follow. Except for that, the area was silent and desolate, and the charred bodies lay all night under the stars, and all the next day. Many people said they heard a hammering noise from the pit area.

That was the state of things on Friday night. In the center, sticking into the skin of our old planet Earth like a poisoned dart, was this cylinder. But the poison was just starting to seep out. Around it were silent fields, still burning in places, and with a few dark, dimly seen objects lying in contorted positions here and there. Scattered about, you could see a burning bush or tree. Beyond that was a fringe of excitement, but the poison's inflammation had not yet passed beyond that fringe. In the rest of the world, the stream of life still flowed as it had flowed for countless years. The fever of war that would soon clog vein and artery, deaden nerve and destroy brain, would still take time to develop.

All night long, the Martians were hammering and stirring, sleepless, tireless, at work on the machines they were constructing, and every once in a while, a puff of greenish-white smoke whirled up into the starlit sky.

About eleven, a company of soldiers came and deployed along the south edge of the fields to form a fighting line. Later, a second company marched through to deploy on the north side. The colonel in command came to the bridge and was busy questioning the crowd at midnight. The military authorities were certainly aware of the seriousness of the business.

A few seconds after midnight, the crowd saw a star fall from heaven into the woods to the northwest. It had a greenish color, and caused a silent brightness like summer lightning. The second cylinder had arrived!

# CHAPTER 8

# The Fighting Begins

**SATURDAY** lives in my memory as a day of suspense. I had slept only a little, and I got up early. I went out into my front yard before breakfast and listened, but I could hear nothing stirring from the direction of the sand pits.

The milkman came as usual. I heard the rattle of his cart, and I went over to the side gate to ask the latest news. He told me that during the night the Martians had been surrounded by troops, and that artillery cannons were expected to arrive soon. Then—a familiar, reassuring note—I heard a train running over near the town.

"They aren't to be killed," said the milkman, "if it can be avoided."

I saw my neighbor gardening, chatted with him for a time, and then strolled in to breakfast. It was a most unexceptional morning. My neighbor was of opinion that the troops would be able to capture or destroy the Martians during the day.

"It's a pity they make themselves so unapproachable," he said. "It would be interesting to know how they live on another planet; we might learn a thing or two."

He came up to the fence and extended a handful of strawberries—his gardening was as generous as it was enthusiastic. He then told me that some of the woods to our north were on fire, "They say that there's another of those blessed things there—number two. But surely one's enough. This trouble will cost the insurance people a pretty penny before everything's settled." He laughed with an air of the greatest good humor as he said this. The northern woods were still burning, he said, and pointed toward a haze of smoke. "That area will be hot for days, on account of the thick soil of pine needles and turf," he said, and then grew serious over "those poor folk that got burned up."

After breakfast, instead of working, I decided to walk down and see what was happening. Under the railway bridge I found a group of soldiers—men in small round caps, dirty, unbuttoned red jackets, blue shirts, dark trousers, and marching boots. They told me no one was allowed over the canal, and, looking along the road toward the bridge, I saw another soldier standing guard. I talked with these soldiers for a time; I told them of my experience the previous afternoon. None of them had seen any Martians, and they plied me with questions. I described the Heat Ray to them, and they began to argue among themselves.

"Crawl up under cover and rush 'em, says I," offered one man.

"Get that!" said another. "What's cover against this here Heat Ray? It'll cook ya! What we got to do is to go as near as the cover will let us, and then dig a trench."

"Trenches! You always want trenches; you ought to have been born a rabbit!"

"They ain't got any necks?" said a third, abruptly. He was a little, dark man, smoking a pipe.

I repeated my description.

"Octopuses," he said, "that's what I'm gonna call 'em. Talk about fishers of men—fighters of fish it is this time!"

"It ain't no murder killing beasts like that," said the first speaker.

"Why not shell the darned things right off and finish 'em?" said the little dark man. "You can't tell what they might do."

"Where's your shells?" said the first speaker. "There ain't no time. Do it in a rush, that's my advice, and do it all at once."

The conversation looked like it would continue along this line, so I left them and went on to the railway station to get a few different morning papers.

The Martians did not come out of the pit where we could see them. They stayed busy, and there was the constant sound of hammering and an almost continuous streamer of smoke. "Fresh attempts have been made to communicate, but without success," was the headline in one of the papers. An officer told me about one of his men getting close to them in a ditch and then waving a flag on a long pole. The Martians took as much notice as we would of the mooing of a cow.

I must confess that the sight of all this armament and all this preparation of men and equipment made me feel better. My imagination became belligerent and defeated the invaders in a dozen striking ways. It hardly seemed like it would be a fair fight at that time. The Martians seemed helpless in their pit.

About three o'clock we heard the firing of a cannon from the north. I learned that the forest where the second cylinder had fallen was being shelled, in the hope of destroying the thing before it opened. It was about five, however, when a field gun finally reached us for use against the first body of Martians.

About six in the evening, as I sat with my wife talking about the upcoming battle, I heard a muffled detonation followed immediately by the noise of small arms fire. This was followed by a violent rattling crash that shook the ground! I ran out on the lawn and saw the tops of the trees to my left burst into smoky red flame, and the tower of our little church slide down into ruin. One of my chimneys cracked as if a shell had hit it, and some masonry came clattering down the roof tiles and made a heap of broken fragments on the flower bed.

My wife joined me, and we stood there in amazement. Then I realized that we were within range of the Martian's Heat Ray! I gripped my wife's arm, and without ceremony ran her out into the road.

"We can't possibly stay here," I said, and as I spoke the firing started up again.

"But where are we to go?" cried my wife in terror.

I couldn't think clearly with all the noise and destruction going on all around me. Then I remembered my cousin who lived close by in Smithville.

"Smithville!" I shouted above the noise.

She looked away from me downhill. The people were coming out of their houses, astonished. She asked, "How are we going to get to Smithville?"

"Stay here! I will be right back!" I commanded, and I started off for the local stable, where I knew the manager. I found him in his office, unaware of what was going on just a mile away.

Because he didn't know what was happening, I was able to borrow a horse and cart after paying only a small fee. I drove it back to our house, and rushed inside and packed a few valuables. The beech trees across the way were burning, and the tall fence up the road glowed red. While I was occupied, a soldier came running up. He was going from house to house, warning people to leave. As I came out of my front door, lugging my treasures tied up in a tablecloth, I shouted: "What is happening?"

He turned, stared, yelled something about "crawling out in a thing like a dish cover," and took off up the road. I ran to the cart, grabbed the reins and jumped up into the driver's seat beside my wife. In another moment, we were clear of the smoke, and moving quickly down the hill away from the noise and fire.

In front of us was a quiet sunny landscape, wheat fields ahead on either side of the road, and a neatly kept farmhouse. At the bottom of the hill, I turned my head to look at the hillside I was leaving. Thick streamers of smoke shot with threads of red fire were driving up into the still air, and throwing dark shadows on the green treetops. The smoke already extended far away to the east and west. The road was dotted with people running toward us. And very faint now, but very distinct through the hot, quiet air, I heard the whirr of a machinegun and the intermittent cracking of rifles. Apparently, the Martians were setting fire to everything within range of their

Heat Ray, and the soldiers were fighting back.

I am not an expert driver, so I had to turn my attention back to the horse. When I looked back again, the second hill had hidden the smoke from the fires. I slashed the horse with the whip, and gave him a loose rein as we drove away in terror.

# CHAPTER 9

# In the Storm

**SMITHVILLE** is about twelve miles from our town. The heavy firing that had broken out while we were driving away, ceased as abruptly as it began, leaving the evening very peaceful and still. We got to there about nine o'clock, and the horse had an hour's rest while I ate supper with my cousin and left my wife in his care.

During the drive, my wife was silent and seemed depressed with forebodings of evil. I talked to her, pointing out that the Martians were confined to the sand pit by sheer heaviness, and at the most could only crawl out of it a little way; but she answered only in monosyllables. Had it not been for my promise to the stable manager to return his horse and cart, she would have urged me to stay in Smithville that night. I wish that I had!

For my own part, I had been excited all day. Something like war fever was in my blood, and in my heart, I was not sorry that I had to return that night. I was even afraid that that last volley of shots I had heard might mean the extermination of our invaders from Mars. I can best describe my state of mind by saying that I wanted to be in at the kill.

It was nearly eleven when I started back. The night was unexpectedly dark; to me, walking out of the lighted passage of my cousin's house, it seemed black, hot, and still. Overhead the clouds were moving fast, although not a breath stirred the shrubs around us. My wife stood in the light of the doorway, and watched me as I drove out of sight.

I was anxious because of my wife's fears, but soon my thoughts went to the Martians. I did not know anything about the afternoon's fighting. As I drove back, I saw along the western horizon, a blood-red glow, which as I drew nearer, crept slowly up into the sky. The driving clouds of the gathering thunderstorm mingled with masses of black and red smoke.

As I approached my town, I was in a valley and did not see much. As I went up the hill, the glare came into view again, and the trees around me shivered with the first hints of the storm that was about to burst. A lurid green glare lit the road in front of me and showed the distant woods. I felt a tug at the reins and looked up. I saw a thread of green fire falling into a nearby field. It was the third falling star!

Immediately afterward, and blindingly violent by contrast, flashed the first bolt of lightning of the gathering storm, and the thunder burst like a cannon. The horse took the bit between his teeth and bolted.

Once the lightning began, it went on in as rapid a succession of flashes as I have ever seen. The thunderclaps, one on the heels of another and with a strange crackling accompaniment, sounded more like the working of a gigantic electric machine than the usual detonating reverberations. The flickering light was blinding and confusing, and suddenly rain hit my face as I galloped down the slope.

At first I noticed little but the road in front of me, but then my attention was drawn to something that was moving rapidly down the opposite slope of the hill. At first I took it for the wet roof of a house, but one flash following another showed it to be in swift rolling movement. It was an elusive vision—a moment of bewildering darkness, and then, in a flash like daylight, the red masses of the buildings near the crest of the hill, the green tops of the pine trees, and this weird thing came out clear and sharp and bright.

And this thing I saw! How can I describe it? It looked like a monstrous tripod, higher than the houses, striding over the young pine trees, smashing them aside. It was a walking machine of glittering metal, striding now across a field; articulate ropes of steel dangling from it, and the clattering tumult of its passage mingling with the riot of the thunder. A vivid flash, heeling over with one leg in the air, to vanish and reappear almost instantly, with the next flash, a hundred yards nearer. Can you imagine a milking stool tilted and moving its legs as it traveled along the ground? That was the impression those instant flashes gave. But instead of a milking stool, imagine an immense piece of machinery on a tripod stand one hundred feet high.

Then, suddenly, the trees in the woods ahead of me spread apart, just like brittle reeds parted by a man stamping through them. They were snapped off and driven apart, and a second huge tripod appeared, rushing right at me! And I was galloping straight at it! At the sight of the second monster, my nerve left me completely. I wrenched the horse's head hard to the right, and in another moment the cart heeled over; the shafts smashed, and I was flung sideways and fell into a shallow pool of water.

I crawled out and crouched in the water, next to a bush. The horse lay motionless (his neck was broken, poor brute!) and by the lightning flashes, I saw the black bulk of the overturned cart and the silhouette of a wheel still spinning slowly. In another moment, the colossal mechanism went striding by me, and passed uphill toward the east.

Seen from close range, the thing was incredibly strange, for it was no mere machine moving along. It was a machine, no doubt about it, with ringing metallic noises, and long, flexible, glittering tentacles (one of which gripped a young pine tree) swinging and rattling around its strange body. As it went striding along, the large hood at the top moved to and fro with the suggestion of a head looking around. Behind the main body was a huge mass of white metal like a gigantic fisherman's basket, and puffs of green smoke squirted out from the joints of the legs as the monster swept by me. In an instant, it was gone.

As it passed, it let loose a deafening howl that drowned out the thunder—"Aloo! Aloo!" And in another moment, it joined up with its companion, half a mile away, stooping over something in the field. I had no doubt that they were standing over the third of the ten cylinders they had fired at us from Mars.

For some minutes, I stayed there in the rain and darkness watching these monstrous beings of metal moving in the distance. The rain was beginning again, and as it came, their figures grew misty but occasionally flashed clear again. Now and then the lightning paused, and the night swallowed them up.

I was soaked. It was some time before my astonishment would let me struggle up the bank to a drier position or think about my imminent peril. Not far from me was a little one-roomed squatter's hut, surrounded by a patch of potato garden. I struggled to my feet, and crouching and making use of every chance of cover, made a run for it. I hammered at the door, but I could not make the people hear (if there were any people inside), and after a time I stopped, and, using a ditch for the greater part of the way, succeeded in crawling into the woods.

I pushed on toward my own house under the cover of the forest. It was very dark in the woods, and the rain, which was pouring down in a torrent, fell in columns through the gaps in the heavy foliage.

If I had better understood the things I had seen, I would have immediately gone back to rejoin my wife at Smithville. But that night, the strangeness of things around me, and my physical wretchedness, stopped me. I was bruised, weary, wet to the skin, and blinded by the storm.

I staggered through the trees, fell into a ditch, and finally splashed out into the lane that ran toward my place. The storm was so heavy that I had a terrible time just making my way up the hill.

Nothing was burning on the hillside, though from the surrounding fields there was still a red glare and a rolling tumult of smoke beating up against the drenching rain. As far as I could see by the flashes, the houses around me were mostly undamaged.

Down the road there was the sound of voices, but I did not have the courage to shout or to go over to them. I found my house and let myself in, locked and bolted the door, staggered to the foot of the staircase, and sat down. My imagination was full of those metallic monsters striding across the countryside. I crouched at the foot of the staircase with my back to the wall, shivering violently.

CHAPTER 10

# At the Window

**AFTER** a time I discovered that I was cold and wet, with little pools of water around me on the carpet. I got up almost mechanically, went into the dining room, drank some whiskey, and then changed my clothes.

After that, I went upstairs to my study where the window looks out over the trees toward the center of town. The hallway was dark, and, by contrast with the picture the window frame enclosed, the side of the room seemed impenetrably dark. I stopped short in the doorway and just looked out.

The thunderstorm had passed. Very far away, lit by a vivid red glare, the fields around the sand pits were visible. Across the light, huge black shapes, grotesque and strange, moved busily to and fro in the pits.

It seemed as if the whole country in that direction was on fire—the broad hillside was alight with little tongues of flame, swaying and writhing with the gusts of the dying storm, and throwing a red reflection on the clouds above. Every now and then, a haze of smoke from some nearer conflagration drove across the window and hid the Martian shapes. I could not see what they were doing, nor could I see the monsters clearly.

I crept toward the window. There was light down the hill by the railway, and several of the houses along the road near the station were glowing ruins. The light at the railway station puzzled me at first; there was a black heap engulfed in smoke and flames and to the right of that was a row of yellow shapes. Then I saw that this was a wrecked train, the front part smashed and on fire, the rear carriages still sitting on the rails.

Between these three points of light—the houses, the train, and the burning countryside—stretched irregular patches of dark country, broken here and there by intervals of dimly glowing and smoking ground. It was a strange spectacle, that black expanse lit up randomly with fires. At first I could see no people at all, though I looked all over. Later, I saw by the light at the train station, a number of shadowy figures hurrying one after the other.

This was the little peaceful world where I had been living for years! This fiery chaos! What had happened in the last seven hours I did not know. Neither did I know, though I was beginning to guess, the relationship between these mechanical monsters and the sluggish lumps I had seen come out of the cylinder. I turned my desk chair to the window, sat down, and stared at the blackened country, and particularly at the three gigantic tripod things that were going to and fro in the glare around the sand pits.

They seemed amazingly busy. I began to ask myself what they could be. Were they intelligent mechanisms? Such a thing I felt was impossible. Or did a Martian sit inside directing, using, controlling . . . like a man's brain sits and rules in his body? I began to compare the things to human machines and to ask myself how an ironclad warship or a steam engine would seem to a lower animal.

The storm had left the sky clear, and over the smoke of the burning land the little fading pinpoint of Mars was dropping into the west. I heard a slight scraping at the fence, and getting up, looked down and saw a soldier climbing over the fence. At the sight of another human being, I leaned out of the window eagerly.

"Hiss!" I whispered.

He stopped next to the fence. Then he came over across the lawn to the house and whispered back, "Who's there?" as he stood under the window, looking up.

"Where are you going?" I asked.

"God knows."

"Are you trying to hide?"

"You guessed it!"

"Come into the house," I said.

I went down, unfastened the door, and let him in, and locked the door again. I could not see his face.

"My God! My God!" he said, as he came in.

"What happened?" I asked.

"What hasn't?" In the dimness I could see he made a gesture of despair. "They wiped us out—simply wiped us out." He repeated this again and again.

He followed me, almost mechanically, into the dining room.

"Take some whiskey," I said, pouring out a stiff dose.

He drank it. Then abruptly sat down, put his head on his arms, and began to sob like a little boy.

It was a long time before he could steady his nerves enough to answer my questions. He was with the artillery, and said the action started in the late afternoon. They were firing across the fields, and he was told the first party of Martians were crawling slowly toward the second cylinder under cover of a metal shield.

Later, this shield staggered up on tripod legs and became the first of the tripod fighting machines. His gun had been set to cover the sand pits, and its arrival was what started the action. In the excitement, he stepped in a rabbit hole and fell. At the same moment, his cannon exploded, the ammunition blew up, and there was fire all around him. A moment later, he found himself lying under a heap of charred dead men and dead horses.

"I lay still," he said, "scared out of my wits, with part of a horse on top of me. We'd been wiped out. And the smell—good God! Like burnt meat! I was stunned by the fall, and I had to lie there until I felt better. We looked just like a parade a minute before—then stumble, bang, swish!"

"Wiped out!" he said again.

He hid under the dead horse for a long time, peering out across the field. Other soldiers had tried to rush the Martian's pit, and were simply swept out of existence. Then the monster had risen to its feet and began to walk leisurely to and fro across the field among the few survivors, with its head-like hood turning exactly like the head of a hooded human being. A kind of arm carried the Heat Ray device and every once in a while it would blast out its mystery ray, and something would burst into flames.

In a few minutes, there was no other living thing left on the field, and every bush and tree around was burning. He heard the Martians rattle around for a time and then become still. The monster saved the railway station and the cluster of houses around it until last; then in a moment the Heat Ray was brought to bear, and the area became a heap of fiery ruins. The thing then shut off the Heat Ray, and began to waddle away toward the smoldering woods that sheltered the second cylinder. As it did so, a second glittering Titan raised itself up out of the pit.

The second monster followed the first, and the soldier began to crawl away over the hot ash. He managed to get into the ditch by the side of the road, and so escaped. He hid among some heaps of broken wall, as one of the Martian giants returned. He saw this one pursue a man, catch him up in one of its steely tentacles, and knock his head against the trunk of a tree.

Since then, he had been skulking along in the direction of London. He had been consumed with thirst until he found a broken water main near the railway arch with the water bubbling out onto the road.

That was the story I got from him, bit by bit. He grew calmer as he told his story and tried to make me see the things he had seen. He had eaten no food since midday and I found some mutton and bread in the pantry and brought it into the room. We did not light a lamp for fear of attracting the Martians. As we talked and ate, I noticed his face, blackened and haggard, as no doubt mine was as well.

When we finished eating, we went upstairs to my study, and I looked out the open window again. In one night, the valley had become a valley of ashes. The fires had dwindled now. Where flames had been there were now streamers of smoke; but the countless ruins of shattered and gutted houses and blasted and blackened trees that the night had hidden, stood out now gaunt and terrible in the pitiless light of dawn. And shining with the growing light of the east, three of the metallic giant fighting machines stood around the pit, their cowls rotating as though they were surveying the desolation they had made.

**CHAPTER 11**

# What I Saw of the Destruction

**AS** the dawn grew brighter, we moved away from the window and went downstairs. The soldier agreed with me that the house was not safe, and we should move on. He wanted to go to London and rejoin his unit. My plan was to return to Smithville, pick up my wife, get to the nearest port, and leave the country as soon as possible—the power of the Martian war machines over our puny forces scared me to death. I knew that the area around London would be the scene of a disastrous struggle before these powerful creatures could be destroyed.

However, the third cylinder, with its giant, protective group of tripod fighting machines, was between Smithville and us. If I was alone, I would have taken my chances and struck out across the country. But the soldier said: "It would not be kind to your lovely wife to make her a widow in the next few days." In the end, I agreed to go with him through the woods, northward around the Martians before we separated, and then I made my way to Smithville.

I would have started out at once, but my military-trained companion knew better than that. He made me ransack the house for flasks, which we filled with whiskey, and jugs that we filled with water. We lined every available pocket with packets of biscuits and slices of meat and any other food we could stuff in. Then we crept out of the house and ran as quickly as we could down the road to the north. The houses we passed seemed deserted. We passed by a group of three charred bodies, struck dead by the Heat Ray; and here and there were things that the fleeing people had dropped—a clock, a slipper, a silver spoon, and similar items.

Except for one or two dwellings, none of the houses had suffered very much out here away from downtown. The Heat Ray had shaved off the chimney tops and passed on. Yet, except for us, there did not seem to be a living soul around. The majority of the inhabitants had escaped—or they were hiding from the monsters.

We went down the lane and entered the woods at the foot of the hill. We pushed through toward the railway without meeting a soul. The woods across the rail line were now scarred and blackened ruins; for the most part, the trees had fallen, but a few still stood, dismal gray stems with dark brown foliage instead of green.

On our side, the fire had done no more than scorch the trees. In one place, the woodsmen had been at work; trees, felled and freshly trimmed, lay in a clearing, with heaps of sawdust left by the sawing-machine and its engine. There was not a breath of wind this morning, and everything was strangely still. Even the birds were hushed, and as we hurried along we talked in whispers and looked frequently over our shoulders. Once or twice we stopped to listen.

After a time, we got near the road, and as we did so, we heard the clatter of hoofs and saw three cavalry soldiers riding slowly south. We called to them, and they stopped. It was a lieutenant and a couple of privates.

"You are the first men I've seen coming this way this morning," said the lieutenant. "What's brewing?"

His voice and face were eager. The men behind him stared at us curiously. My companion scrambled onto the road and saluted.

"Gun destroyed last night, sir. Have been hiding. Trying to rejoin battery, sir. You'll come in sight of the Martians, I expect, about half a mile along this road."

"What the dickens are they like?" asked the lieutenant.

"Giants in armor, sir. Hundred feet high.

Three legs and a body like aluminum, with a large hood on top, sir."

"Get out!" scoffed the lieutenant. "What confounded nonsense!"

"You'll see, sir. They carry a kind of box, sir, that shoots fire and strikes you dead."

"What do you mean—a gun?"

"No, sir," and the soldier began a vivid account of the Heat Ray. Halfway through, the lieutenant interrupted him and looked up at me. I was still standing on the bank by the side of the road.

"It's perfectly true," I said.

"Well," said the lieutenant, "I suppose it's my business to go up and see it, too. Look," he said to my companion, "we're here to clear people out of their houses. You'd better go along, and report yourself to the general. Tell him all you know. He's camped up the road about two miles north."

He turned his horse southward again and said, "Half a mile, you say?"

"At most," I answered, and pointed over the treetops southward. He thanked me and rode on, and we did not see them again.

After a while, we emerged from the trees and found the country calm and peaceful under the morning sunlight. We were far beyond the range of the Heat Ray, and if it was not for the emptiness of some of the houses, the stirring movement of packing in others, and the knot of soldiers standing on the bridge over the railway and staring south, the day would have seemed like any other Sunday.

Several farm wagons and carts were moving along the road, and through the gate of a field, we saw across a stretch of flat meadow, six large cannons pointing south. The gunners stood by the guns waiting, and the ammunition wagons were close by. The men stood at attention like they were in a parade.

"That's good!" I said. "They will get out one fair shot, at any rate."

Farther north, just over the bridge, there were a number of men in fatigue jackets building a barrier to protect more large guns.

"It's bows and arrows against the lightning, anyhow," said my companion. "They haven't seen that Heat Ray yet."

The officers who were not actively engaged, stood and stared over the treetops toward the south, and the men digging would stop every now and then to stare in the same direction.

The town was in a tumult; people packing and shouting and running around, and a score of soldiers were herding them along. Three or four government wagons, among other vehicles, were being loaded in the village street. There were more than fifty people grouped around the wagons. The soldiers were having a hard time making them realize the gravity of their position. We saw one old fellow with a huge box and a score of flower pots containing orchids, arguing with the corporal who told him to leave them behind. I stopped and gripped his arm.

"Do you know what's over there?" I said, pointing at the treetops that hid the Martians.

"Eh?" said he, turning. "I was explaining that these are valuable!"

"Death!" I shouted. "Death is coming! Death!" and leaving him to digest that, I hurried on after my companion. At the corner, I looked back. The soldier had left the old man, and he was still standing by his box, with the pots of orchids, and staring vaguely over the trees.

No one in town could tell us where the general's headquarters were. The whole place was in such confusion! Carts and carriages were everywhere. The town's inhabitants, men in golf and boating costumes, and their wives in pretty Sunday dresses, were packing up and preparing to evacuate. The children were highly delighted at this astonishing variation of their Sunday routine. In the midst of it all, the village preacher was holding an early service, and his bell was jangling out above the excitement.

My companion and I, seated next to a fountain, made a very passable meal with what we had brought with us. Patrols of soldiers were warning people to move out of town or to hide in their cellars as soon as the firing began. We saw that a growing crowd of people had assembled around the railway station, and the swarming platform was piled with boxes and packages. The ordinary rail traffic had been stopped in order to allow for the passage of troops and guns. I heard that savage struggles occurred for places in the special trains that ran at a later hour.

We remained in town until midday, and on our way out on the ferry we found an excited and noisy crowd of fugitives. The flight had not yet grown to a panic, but there were already far more people than all the boats going to and fro could carry over the river any time soon.

There was a lot of shouting, and one man was even jesting. These people seemed to think that the Martians were simply formidable human beings, who might attack and sack the town, but would be destroyed in the end. Every now and then people would glance nervously toward the south, but everything in that direction seemed still.

After we got across the river, everything was quiet, in vivid contrast with our side. The people who landed there from the boats went tramping off down the lane.

Then a sound came from the south, a muffled thud—the sound of a gun.

The fighting was beginning. Almost immediately, unseen artillery batteries across the river to our right—unseen because of the trees—took up the chorus, firing heavily one after the other. A woman screamed. Everyone seemed stopped by the sudden stir of battle, near us and yet invisible to us. Nothing could be seen except flat meadows and large trees motionless in the warm sunlight.

"The soldiers will stop them," said a woman beside me, doubtfully. A haziness rose over the treetops.

Then suddenly, we saw a rush of smoke far away up the river, a puff of smoke that jerked up into the air and hung; and then the ground heaved under foot and a heavy explosion shook the air, smashing two or three windows in the houses nearby, and leaving us astonished.

"Here they are!" shouted a man in a blue jersey. "Over there! Do you see them? Over yonder!"

Quickly, one after the other, one, two, three, four of the tall armored Martian fighting machines appeared, far away over the trees, across the flat meadows that stretched toward the south. They seemed like little stick-like figures at first, moving along with a rolling motion and going as fast as flying birds.

Then, advancing directly toward us, came a fifth monster. Their armored bodies glittered in the sun as they swept swiftly forward toward the guns, growing rapidly larger as they came nearer. One, on the extreme left, held a huge case high in the air, and the ghostly, terrible Heat Ray I had already seen on Friday night moved to the north and struck the town.

At the sight of these strange, swift, and terrible creatures, the crowd near the water's edge seemed to be horror-struck. There was no screaming or shouting, but a silence. Then a hoarse murmur and a movement of feet started. A man, too frightened to drop a large piece of furniture he carried on his shoulder, swung around and hit me with the corner of his burden. A woman shoved me and hurried past. I turned with the rush of the people, but I was not too terrified for thought. The terrible Heat Ray was in my mind. Get under water! That was it!

"Get under water!" I shouted, unheeded.

I turned around again and rushed toward the approaching Martian, rushed right down the gravelly beach and headlong into the water! Others did the same. A boatload of people reaching the shore came leaping out as I rushed past. The stones under my feet were muddy and slippery, and I was in the water waist-deep. Then, as the Martian towered overhead only a couple of hundred yards away, I flung myself forward under the surface.

But the Martian machine took no more notice of the people running this way and that than a man would of an anthill. When I finally raised my head above water, the Martian's hood turned toward the batteries that were still firing across the river, and as it advanced, it pointed the Heat Ray in their direction.

In another moment, it was on the bank, and in a singe stride it was halfway across. The knees of its front legs bent at the far bank, and in another moment it rose to its full height again. Six cannons, hidden behind the outskirts of town, fired simultaneously. The sudden concussion made my heart jump. The monster was already raising the Heat Ray as the first shell burst just above its hood.

I cried out in astonishment. I saw and thought nothing of the other four Martian monsters; my attention was riveted on the one in front of me. Simultaneously, two other shells burst in the air near the body as the hood twisted round in time to receive, but not in time to dodge, the fourth shell.

The shell burst clean in the face of the monster! The hood bulged, flashed, and whirled off in a dozen tattered fragments of red flesh and glittering metal.

"Hit!" I shouted, with something between a scream and a cheer.

I heard answering shouts from the people in the water around me. I felt like I could leap out of the water with that momentary exultation.

The decapitated colossus reeled like a drunken giant; but it did not fall over. It recovered its balance by some miracle and swung the Heat Ray toward the town, blasting away. The once living, intelligent Martian inside the hood, was slain and splashed to the four winds of heaven, but the fighting machine was now out of control, blundering to destruction. It struck the tower of a church, smashing it down, swerved, continued on and collapsed with tremendous force out of my sight.

A violent explosion shook the air, and a spout of water, steam, mud, and shattered metal shot far up into the sky. As the Heat Ray hit the water, the water flashed into steam. In another moment, a huge wave, almost scalding hot, came sweeping round the bend upstream. I saw people struggling toward the shore, and heard their screaming above the seething roar of the Martian's collapse.

For a moment, I paid no attention to the heat and forgot the need of self-preservation. I splashed through the tumultuous water until I could see around the bend. The fallen Martian came into sight downstream, lying across the river, and for the most part submerged.

Thick clouds of steam were pouring off the wreckage, and through the whirling wisps, I could see the gigantic limbs churning the water and flinging up a spray of mud and froth into the air. The tentacles swayed and struck like living arms, and it was like some wounded thing was struggling for its life. Enormous quantities of some brown fluid were spurting up in noisy jets out of the machine.

My attention was drawn away from this death flurry by a furious screaming noise. A man shouted inaudibly to me and pointed. Looking back, I saw the other Martians advancing with gigantic strides down the riverbank. The hidden cannons spoke again, but this time with less astounding results.

I ducked under water again and swam under the surface as long as I could. The water was in a tumult, and rapidly growing hotter. When I raised my head to take a breath, steam was rising in a whirling white fog that hid the Martians completely. The noise was deafening. Then I saw them through the fog, colossal figures of gray, magnified by the mist. They had gone by me, and two were stooping over the frothing, tumultuous ruins of their comrade.

They stood beside the one in the water, one perhaps two hundred yards from me, the other a little farther away. Their Heat Rays waved high, and the hissing beams smote down this way and that.

The air was full of sound, a deafening and confusing conflict of noises—the clangorous din of the Martians, the crash of falling houses, the thud of trees, fences, sheds flashing into flame, and the crackling and roaring of fire. Dense dark smoke was leaping up to mingle with the steam from the river, and as a Heat Ray went to and fro, its impact was marked by flashes of incandescent white that turned into a smoky dance of flames. The nearer houses still stood intact, awaiting their fate, shadowy, faint and pallid in the steam, with the fire behind them roaring up to the sky.

For a moment, I stood there, chest-high in the almost boiling water, dumbfounded at my position, hopeless of escape. I could see some of the people who had been with me in the river scrambling out of the water through the reeds, like little frogs hurrying through grass, away from the advance of a man, or running to and fro in utter dismay as they reached the road.

Then suddenly the white flashes of the Heat Ray came leaping toward me. The houses caved in as they dissolved into flames at its touch; the trees changed to fire with a roar. The Heat Ray flickered up and down the road, licking off the people who ran this way and that, and came down to the water's edge not fifty yards from where I stood. It swept across the river, and the water in its track rose in a boiling wall crested with steam. I moved toward the shore.

In another moment, the huge wave, almost at the boiling point, swept over me. I screamed aloud. Scalded, half-blinded, and in agony, I staggered through the leaping, hissing water toward the shore. I fell helplessly, in full sight of the Martians, on the broad, bare gravelly ramp that runs down to the river. I expected nothing but death.

I have a dim memory of the foot of a Martian coming down within a few yards of my head, driving straight into the loose gravel, whirling it this way and that and lifting again. I saw the four monsters carrying the debris of their comrade between them, now clear, and then faint through a veil of smoke, receding across a vast space of river and meadow. And then, very slowly, I realized that by some miracle, I had escaped.

**CHAPTER 12**

# How I Fell in with the Priest

**AFTER** getting this sudden lesson in the power of terrestrial weapons, the Martians retreated. In their haste, and busy carrying the debris of their smashed companion, they no doubt overlooked many such stray and negligible victims as myself. Had they left their comrade and pushed on, there was nothing between them and London but a few batteries of cannon, and they would certainly have reached the capital in advance of any warning.

But they were in no hurry. Cylinder followed cylinder on its interplanetary flight; every twenty-four hours brought them reinforcements. And meanwhile the authorities, now fully aware of the tremendous power of the invaders, worked with furious energy. Every minute a fresh cannon came into position until, before twilight, every group of trees and every row of suburban villas on the hilly slopes masked a black muzzle.

And through the charred and desolated area—perhaps twenty square miles altogether—that encircled the Martian encampment, through burned and ruined villages, through the blackened and smoking arcades that had been but a day ago pine forests, crawled the devoted military scouts that were to warn the gunners of the Martian approach. But the Martians now understood the danger of artillery and the danger of humans, and no man got within a mile of them, except at the price of his life.

It would seem that the giants spent the earlier part of the afternoon going to and fro, transferring everything from the second and third cylinders to their original sand pit near my little village. Over that, above the blackened heather and ruined buildings that stretched far and wide, one machine stood as a sentinel, while the others went down into the pit. They were hard at work there far into the night, and the towering column of dense green smoke that rose up could be seen from miles away.

And while the Martians were preparing for their next advance, I made my painful way toward London.

I saw an abandoned boat drifting downstream, and I grabbed it and floated away from the destruction. There were no oars in the boat, but I fixed up a paddle as well as my parboiled hands would allow. Going very tediously, and continually looking behind me, as you may well understand, I followed the river downstream, because I thought that the water gave me my best chance of escape if the giant monsters were to return.

The hot water, steam, and mist from the damaged Martian fighting machine drifted downstream with me, so that for the best part of a mile, I could see little of either bank. Once, however, I made out a string of shadowy figures hurrying across the meadows.

Several of the houses facing the river were on fire. It was strange to see everything so tranquil and desolate under the hot blue sky, with the smoke and little threads of flame going straight up into the heat of the afternoon. Never before had I seen houses burning without drawing a crowd. A little farther on, the dry reeds up the bank were smoking and glowing, and a line of fire was marching steadily across a field of hay.

I took off most of my soaked clothes, and for a long time I just drifted. I was so weary after the violence I had been through, that I could barely move. Then my fears got the better of me again, and I resumed my paddling. The sun scorched my bare back. At last my fatigue overcame my fears, and I landed on the bank and lay down, deadly sick, in the long grass. I got up after a while, walked half a mile without meeting a soul, and then lay down again in the shadow of a hedge. My failure to reach Smithville and rejoin my wife worried me, but I just could not move.

I do not remember the arrival of the priest. I became aware of him as a seated figure in a soot-smudged shirt, and with his upturned, clean-shaven face staring at a faint flickering of lightening that danced over the sky.

I sat up, and at the rustle of my motion, he looked at me.

"Do you have any water?" I asked abruptly.

He shook his head.

"You have been asking for water for the last hour," he said.

For a moment we were silent, taking stock of each other. I dare say he found me a strange enough figure, barely dressed in only my water-soaked pants and socks, scalded, and my face and shoulders blackened by smoke. His face was fair, his chin retreated, and his hair lay in crisp, almost flaxen curls on his low forehead; his eyes were rather large, pale blue, and blankly staring. He spoke abruptly, looking vacantly away from me.

"What does it mean?" he said. "What do these things mean?"

I stared at him and could not answer.

He spoke in almost a complaining tone, "Why are these things permitted? What sins have we done? The morning service was over, I was walking along the road to clear my brain for the afternoon, and then—fire, earthquake, death! As if it were Sodom and Gomorrah! All our work undone, all the work—What are these Martians?"

"What are we?" I answered, clearing my throat.

He gripped his knees and turned to look at me again. For half a minute, perhaps, he stared silently.

"I was walking to clear my brain," he said. "And suddenly—fire, earthquake, death! All the work—all the Sunday schools—What have we done—what has our quiet little town done? Everything gone—everything destroyed. The church! We rebuilt it only three years ago. Gone! Swept out of existence! Why?"

Another pause, and he broke out again like one demented, "The smoke of her burning goeth up for ever and ever!" he shouted. His eyes flamed, and he pointed a lean finger toward the south.

By this time, I was beginning to figure him out. The tremendous tragedy in which he had been involved—it was evident he was a fugitive from the destroyed town—had driven him to the very edge of his reason.

"Are we far from London?" I asked in a matter-of-fact tone.

"What are we to do?" he responded, ignoring me completely. "Are these creatures everywhere? Have they taken over the Earth?"

"Are we far from London?"

"Only this morning I officiated at the early service . . ."

"Things have changed," I said, quietly. "You must keep your head. There is still hope."

"Hope!"

"Yes. Hope—in spite of all this destruction!"

I began to explain my view of our position. He listened at first, but as I went on the interest dawning in his eyes gave way to their former stare, and his attention wandered from me.

"This must be the beginning of the end," he said, interrupting me. "The end! The great and terrible day of the Lord! When men shall call up to the mountains and the rocks fall upon them and hide them—hide them from the face of Him that sitteth upon the throne!"

I began to understand the situation. I stopped my labored reasoning, struggled to my feet, and, standing over him, laid my hand on his shoulder.

"Be a man!" I said firmly. "You are scared out of your wits! What good is religion if it collapses under calamity? Think of what earthquakes and floods, wars and volcanoes, have done to men before! Did you think God had exempted your little town? He is not an insurance agent."

He sat in silence for a while before asking, "But how can we escape? They are invulnerable, they are pitiless."

"Neither the one nor, perhaps, the other," I answered. "And the mightier they are the more sane and wary we should be. One of them was killed back toward the south not three hours ago."

"Killed!" he said, staring about him. "How can God's ministers be killed?"

"I saw it happen." I proceeded to tell him. "We happened to be in the middle of the battle, that's all."

"What is that flicker in the sky?" he asked abruptly.

I told him it was our army's signaling lights—that it was the sign of human help and effort in the sky. I continued, "We are in the midst of it, quiet as it is. That flicker in the sky tells of the gathering storm. Yonder, I take it, are the Martians, and toward London, where those hills rise and the trees give cover, earthworks are being thrown up and guns are being placed. Soon the Martians will be coming this way again."

And even as I spoke, he sprang to his feet and stopped me with a gesture and a shout, "Listen!"

From beyond the low hills across the water came the dull thud of distant guns and a remote, weird crying. Then everything was still. High in the west, the crescent moon hung faint and pale above the smoke and the hot, still splendor of the sunset.

"We had better follow this path to the north," I said as I started off toward London.

**CHAPTER 13**

# In London

**MY** younger brother was in London when the Martians first landed. He was a medical student and was busy studying for an important examination, so he heard nothing of the Martian arrival until Saturday morning. The morning papers on Saturday contained, in addition to lengthy special articles on the planet Mars, a brief and vaguely-worded article about the first attack by the Martians in my hometown.

The article stated that, alarmed by the approach of a crowd, the invaders had killed a number of people with a quick-firing gun. It ended with the words: "Formidable as they seem to be, the Martians have not moved away from the pit where they initially landed, and, indeed, seem incapable of doing so. Probably, this is due to the relative strength of the Earth's gravitational pull compared to that on Mars."

Of course, all the students were intensely interested, but there were no signs of any unusual excitement in the streets. The afternoon papers wrote scraps of news under big headlines. They had nothing to tell beyond the movements of troops and the burning of the woods south of the city. Later, in extra-special late night editions, they announced the interruption of telegraph communication. This was thought to be due to the falling of burning trees across the line. Nothing more of the fighting was known that night, the night of my drive to Smithville and back.

My brother felt no anxiety about us, since he knew from the description in the papers that the cylinder was a good two miles from my house. He made up his mind to come down and visit me to see the things before they were killed. He sent a telegram, which never reached me, detailing his plans.

As he waited on the train platform, he learned that some kind of accident or breakdown prevented trains from reaching my area that night. Few people, except for the railway officials, connected the breakdown with the Martians.

About five o'clock, the gathering crowd in the station was excited by the passage of a train pulling flatcars loaded with huge cannons and carriages crammed full of soldiers. There was an exchange of pleasantries: "You'll get eaten!" "We're the beast-tamers!" "Go get 'em, boys!" and so forth. A little while after that, a squad of police came into the station explaining the emergency and began to clear the public off the platforms, and my brother went out into the street again.

Outside, he saw a couple of newsboys who had just rushed out with fresh newspapers. "Dreadful catastrophe!" they shouted down the street. "Fighting to the South! Full description! Repulse of the Martians! London in Danger!" He quickly bought a copy.

Then, and only then, did he realize something of the full power and terror of these monsters. He learned that they were not merely a handful of small sluggish creatures, but that they were minds controlling vast mechanical bodies; and that they could move swiftly and strike with such power that even the mightiest guns could not stand against them.

They were described as "vast, tripod-legged machines, nearly a hundred feet high, capable of the speed of an express train, and able to shoot out a beam of intense heat." The newspaper described massed artillery batteries that had been planted in the south country to protect London. Five of the machines had been seen moving toward the river, and one, by a happy chance, had been destroyed. In the other cases, the shells had missed, and the terrible Heat Rays had annihilated the batteries. Heavy losses of soldiers were mentioned, but the tone of the dispatch was optimistic.

The Martians had been repulsed; they were not invulnerable. They had retreated to their southern base. Scouts were pushing toward them from all sides. Cannon and other armament and troops were in rapid transit from bases all over the country. Altogether, one hundred and sixteen were in position or being hastily placed, mainly covering the approaches to London. Never before in England had there been such a vast concentration of military material.

Any further cylinders that fell, it was hoped, could be destroyed at once by high explosives, which were being rapidly manufactured and distributed. The government described the situation as strange and grave, but the public was urged to avoid panic. No doubt, the Martians were terrible, but there were very few of them against our millions.

The authorities had reason to suppose, from the size of the cylinders, that there could not be more than five Martians in each cylinder. And one fighting machine at least had been killed—perhaps more. The public would be properly notified of the approach of danger, and elaborate measures were being taken for the protection of the people in the threatened southern suburbs. And so, with reiterated assurances of the safety of London, and the ability of the authorities to cope with the difficulty, the article ended.

This news was very exciting to the people on the streets, whatever their previous apathetic thoughts on the matter might have been. The shutters of a map shop were being taken down, and a man was visible inside the window hastily fastening maps of the southern suburbs to the glass.

Going along with the paper in his hand, my brother saw some of the fugitives from the recent conflict. There was a man with his wife and two boys and some articles of furniture in a cart. He was coming from the south; and close behind him came a hay wagon with five or six respectable-looking people. The faces of these people were haggard, and their appearance contrasted with the Sunday-best appearance of the people around them on the street. People in fashionable clothing peered at them out of cabs. They stopped as if undecided which way to go, and finally turned eastward. Some way behind these folks came a man in workday clothes, riding a bicycle. He was dirty and white in the face.

My brother turned south and met a number of such people. He had a vague idea that he might see me among these people. He noticed an unusual number of police regulating the traffic. Some of the refugees were exchanging news with the people on the street. One said he had actually seen the Martians, "Boiler tanks on stilts, I tell you, striding along like men."

Further south, the bars were doing a lively trade with these arrivals. At all the street corners, groups of people were reading papers and talking excitedly or staring at these unusual Sunday visitors. My brother said the flow of people seemed to increase as it got later, until at last, the roads were packed with humanity. He talked with several of these fugitives and got unsatisfactory answers from most of them. No one could tell him any news about my neighborhood except one man, who assured him my entire town had been entirely destroyed on the previous night.

"I come from close by there," he said; "a man on a bicycle came through the place in the early morning and went from door to door warning us to run away. Then came soldiers. We went out to look, and there were clouds of smoke to the south—nothing but smoke. Then we heard the guns and saw folks coming our way. So I've locked up my house and come here."

At the time, there was a strong feeling in the streets that the authorities were to blame for their incapacity to take care of the invaders without all this inconvenience.

Later, the noise of heavy firing could be heard all over the south of London. My brother could not hear it well in his neighborhood because of the traffic, but by striking through the quiet back streets to the river, he was able to distinguish it quite plainly.

By the time he walked back to his apartment, he was very worried about me and disturbed by the magnitude of the trouble. His mind seemed to dwell on military details. He thought of all those silent, expectant guns, of the suddenly empty countryside; he tried to imagine "boiler tanks on stilts" a hundred feet high.

He read and re-read the paper, fearing the worst had happened to me. He was restless, and after supper went out to prowl the streets again. He returned and tried to study for his medical exam. He went to bed a little after midnight and was awakened in the small hours of Monday by the sounds of doors slamming, feet running in the street, distant drumming, and a clamor of bells. Red reflections danced on the ceiling. For a moment, he lay there astonished, wondering whether day had come or the world had gone mad. Then he jumped out of bed and ran to the window.

As he stuck his head out, he heard a dozen echoes to the noise of his window sash slamming open, and saw many of his neighbors' heads in every kind of night disarray appear out of other windows. Questions were being shouted. "They are coming!" bawled a policeman, hammering at the door; "the Martians are coming!" and hurried to the next door.

The sound of drumming and trumpeting came from the nearby army barracks, and every church within earshot was hard at work killing sleep with a disorderly ringing of their bells. There was noise of doors opening, and window after window flashed from darkness to illumination.

Galloping up the street came a closed carriage, bursting abruptly into noise at the corner, rising to a clattering climax under the window, and dying away slowly in the distance. Close behind came a couple of cabs, the beginning of a long procession of vehicles, going north for the most part to the train station, where special trains were loading up.

For a long time my brother stared out of the window in astonishment, watching the policemen hammering at door after door, delivering their incomprehensible message. Then the door behind him opened, and the man who lodged across the landing came in, dressed in his pajamas and slippers, his hair disordered from his pillow.

"What the devil is it?" he asked. "A fire? What's all this confounded noise?"

They both craned their heads out of the window, straining to hear what the policemen were shouting. People were coming out of the side streets and standing in groups at the corners.

"What the devil is it all about?" said my brother's fellow lodger.

My brother answered him vaguely and began to dress, running with each garment to the window so he would not miss any of the growing excitement. And soon men selling unnaturally early newspapers came shouting into the street: "London in danger of suffocation! The southern defenses have been overrun! Fearful massacres in the south!"

And all around him—in the rooms below, in the houses on each side and across the road, and all over south London—people were rubbing their eyes, and opening windows to stare out and ask aimless questions, dressing hastily as the first breath of the coming storm of fear blew through the streets. It was the dawn of the great panic. London, which had gone to bed on Sunday night oblivious and inert, was awakened, in the small hours of Monday morning, to a vivid sense of danger.

Unable to learn what was happening from his window, my brother went down to the street just as the sky between the houses grew pink with the early dawn. The people on foot and in vehicles grew more numerous every moment. "Black Smoke!" he heard people crying, and again "Black Smoke!" The spreading panic was inevitable. As my brother hesitated on the doorstep, he saw another news vendor approaching and bought a paper. The man was running away with the rest, and selling his papers for ten times their normal price as he ran—a grotesque mingling of profit and panic.

And from this paper my brother read that catastrophic dispatch of the Commander-in-Chief: "The Martians are able to discharge enormous clouds of a black and poisonous vapor by means of rockets. They have smothered our arti-lary batteries, destroyed many towns in the south, and are advancing slowly toward London, destroying everything on the way. It is impossible to stop them. There is no safety from the black smoke other than instant flight.

That was all, but it was enough. The whole population of London—some six-million peo-ple—was stirring, slipping, running; presently it would be pouring EN MASSE northward.

"Black Smoke!" the voices cried. "Fire!"

The bells of the neighboring church made a jangling tumult. A cart smashed, amid shrieks and curses, against the water trough up the street. Sickly yellow lights went to and fro in the houses, and some of the passing cabs carried rid-ers clinging to the sides and roof in a most unsafe manner. And overhead the dawn was growing brighter, clear and steady and calm.

He heard footsteps running around in the rooms and up and down the stairs behind him. His landlady went to the front door, loosely wrapped in a dressing gown and shawl. Her husband fol-lowed behind, breathing hard, as they both stopped and watched the commotion in the street.

As my brother began to realize the impor-tance of all these things, he returned to his own room, put all his available money—some ten pounds altogether—into his pockets, and went out again into the streets.

## CHAPTER 14

# What Had Happened in the South

**I**T was while the priest and I walked toward London, and while my brother was watching the refugees stream by his street, that the Martians resumed their offensive. Most of them stayed at the original sand pit until later that night preparing another one of their terrible weapons.

But three of them came out about eight o'clock and, advancing slowly and cautiously, made their way north until they came in sight of the waiting artillery batteries. These Martians did not advance together, but spread out in a line, each perhaps a mile and a half from his nearest partner. They communicated with one another by means of siren-like howls, running up and down the scale from one note to another.

This howling and firing of cannon frightened us so much that the priest and I hid under a bridge. The gunners, unseasoned artillery volunteers who should never have been placed in such a position, fired one wild, premature, ineffectual volley, and bolted on horse and foot through the deserted village, while the lead Martian, without using his Heat Ray, walked serenely over their guns, passed in front of them, and came unexpectedly to the next line of defensive cannon which he destroyed.

The flanking battery, hidden in the woods on the right side, however, were better led or better trained. Concealed by the trees, they were not suspected by the Martian as he traveled in front of them. They aimed their guns as carefully as if they had been on the practice field, and fired at about a thousand yards' range.

The shells flashed all round the Martian, and he was seen to advance a few paces, stagger, and go down. Everybody yelled together, and the guns were reloaded in frantic haste. The damaged Martian gave off a loud screaming noise, and immediately a second glittering giant appeared over the trees to the south. One of the legs on the first Martian had been smashed by the cannon fire. The whole of the second volley flew wide of the Martian on the ground, and, simultaneously, both his companions brought up their Heat Rays and aimed at the battery. The ammunition blew up, the trees all around the guns flashed into fire, and only one or two of the men who were already running over the crest of the hill escaped.

After this, it would seem that the three Martians took counsel together and halted, and the scouts who were watching them reported that they remained absolutely stationary for the next half hour. The Martian, whose machine had been damaged, crawled tediously out of his hood-like cockpit and began the repair of his damaged support leg. He finished his task, and the three Martians were seen above the trees again making their way to the north.

It was a few minutes past nine that night, when the three monster machines met up with four other Martians, each carrying a thick metal tube. A similar tube was passed on to each of the three, and the seven proceeded at equal distances along a curved line toward London.

The army scouts fired rockets that flew up over the hills in front of the walking machines as soon as they began to move. These signal flares warned the waiting artillery batteries hiding in the next valley. Four of the alien fighting machines crossed the river, and two of them, dark against the western sky, came into our view as we hurried along the road. It seemed like they moved on a cloud as a milky mist covered the fields and rose to a third of their height.

The priest saw them, cried out faintly, and began to run. I knew it was no good running from a Martian, so I turned and crawled through some nettles and brambles into the ditch by the side of the road. The priest looked back, saw what I was doing, and turned around to join me.

The two monsters halted, the nearer one standing and facing north, the farther one seemed like a gray phantom floating in the mist. The howling of the Martians stopped, and they took up their positions in the long curved battle line. They were each holding their cylinders in absolute silence. It was a crescent-shaped line with twelve miles between its horns. Never since the devising of gunpowder was the beginning of a battle so still. To us, and to any observer around the city, it would have had precisely the same effect—the Martians seemed in solitary possession of the dark night, lit only by the slender moon, the stars, the afterglow of the daylight, and the ruddy glare of the woods to the south.

But facing that crescent everywhere—in the hollow, behind the large barn, next to the white church, behind hills and woods south of the river, and across the flat grass meadows to the north of it, wherever a cluster of trees or village houses gave sufficient cover—the cannons were waiting. The signal rockets burst and rained their sparks through the night and vanished, and the spirit of all those watching batteries rose to a tense expectation. The Martians had only to advance into the line of fire, and instantly, those motionless black forms of men, those guns glittering so darkly in the early night, would explode into the thunderous fury of battle.

No doubt, the thought that was uppermost in a thousand of those vigilant minds, even as it was uppermost in mine, was the riddle—how much they understood of us. Did they grasp that we in our millions were organized, disciplined, working together? Or did they interpret our spurts of fire, the sudden stinging of our shells, our feeble encirclement of their encampment, as we would think of the furious onslaught of a disturbed hive of bees? Did they think they could exterminate us?

A hundred such questions went through my mind as I watched the immense tripod figures. And in the back of my mind was the sense of the unknown and hidden armed forces set up all the way to London. Had they prepared pitfalls? Could our engineers rig the gunpowder factories as some kind of explosive trap? Would the people of London have the heart and courage to set up a defense like those that Moscow set against Napoleon and his French forces?

Then, after what seemed an interminable time, came a sound like the distant concussion of a gun. Another nearer, and then another! And then, the Martian beside us raised his tube and discharged it like a gun, with a heavy report that made the ground heave. The one off to the left answered him. There was no flash, no smoke, simply that loud bang!

I was so shocked by these heavy Martian guns following one after another, that I forgot my personal safety and stood up to look. As I did so, another loud report followed, and a big projectile hurtled overhead. I expected to see smoke or fire, or some such evidence of its work. But all I saw was the deep blue sky above, with one solitary star, and the white mist spreading wide and low beneath. And there had been no crash, no answering explosion. The silence was restored, and I watched and waited. One minute lengthened to three.

"What has happened?" whispered the priest, standing up beside me.

"Heaven only knows!" I replied.

A bat flickered by and vanished. A distant sound of shouting began and then suddenly ceased. I looked up again at the Martian, and saw he was now moving eastward along the riverbank.

Every moment, I expected that some hidden battery of guns would open fire on him; but the evening calm was unbroken. The figure of the Martian grew smaller as he receded, and soon the mist and the gathering night swallowed him up. We climbed up higher to get a better look. Toward our left, we saw a dark form, like a round hill that had suddenly appeared out of nowhere, hiding our view of that part of the country. As we watched, farther across the river, we saw another new summit take shape. These hill-like forms became lower and broader as we stared at them.

Moved by a sudden thought, I looked north-ward, and there I saw that another of these cloudy black shadows had risen up from the level ground.

Everything had suddenly become very still. Far away to the southeast, we heard the Martians hooting to one another, and then the air quiv-ered again with the distant thud of their guns. But our earthly artillery made no reply.

At the time, we could not understand what was happening, but later I was to learn the mean-ing of these mounds that gathered in the twi-light. Each of the Martians, standing in the great crescent I have described, shot one or more large canisters out in front of him. These canisters smashed open when they struck the ground and discharged an enormous volume of heavy, inky vapor, coiling and pouring upward in a huge black cloud. The dark mass became a gaseous hill that rose up and then sank and spread itself slow-ly over the surrounding country. And the touch of that vapor, the inhaling of its pungent wisps, was death to anything that breathes.

The vapor was heavier than the densest smoke, and it poured over the ground in a man-ner more like liquid than gas. It flowed down off any high areas and streamed into the valleys and ditches. It flowed sluggishly down the slope of the land and slowly combined with the mist and moisture of the air. Later, it sank to the earth in the form of dust, a black, powder-like dust that covered everything.

We saw some of this action from the upstairs window of a deserted house. From there, we could see a search light going to and fro, and about eleven, the windows rattled, and we heard the sound of the huge siege guns far off in the distance. These continued intermittently for about a quarter of an hour, sending shots at the invisible Martians, and then the pale beams of the searchlight vanished and were replaced by a bright red glow.

Then the fourth cylinder fell—a brilliant green meteor—as I learned afterward, miles to the west. Before the guns over there began to fire, there was a fitful cannonade far away in the southwest, due, I believe, to guns being fired before the black smoke could overwhelm the gunners.

So, setting about it as methodically as men might smoke out a wasps' nest, the Martians spread this strange stifling vapor over the country to the south of London. The horns of the crescent slowly moved apart, until at last, they formed a line miles across. All night they advanced. After that one Martian was knocked down, they never again gave the artillery a chance against them. Wherever there was a possibility that there might be hidden guns being aimed at them, a fresh canister of the black smoke was discharged, and where our guns were openly displayed, the Heat Ray was used to destroy them.

By midnight, the blazing trees and fields to the south threw their light on a network of black smoke, blotting out the whole valley of the river Thames and extending as far as the eye could reach. And through this, two Martians slowly waded, turning the hoods on top of their fighting machines from one side to another as hissing steam jetted out.

They used the Heat Ray sparingly that night, either because they had only a limited supply of power, or because they did not wish to destroy the country but only to crush and overawe the human opposition. In the latter aim, they certainly succeeded. Sunday night was the end of organized opposition to their movements. After that, no body of men would stand against them—our soldiers knew the fight would be hopeless. Even the crews of the torpedo-boats and destroyers that steamed up the Thames refused to stop and fight. They just turned around and went back downstream again. The only offensive operation men tried after that night was the preparation of mines and pitfalls, and even in that, their energies were frantic and uncoordinated.

One has to imagine the fate of those hidden artillery batteries so carefully placed waiting for the Martians. There were no survivors. One may picture the officers alert and watchful, the gunners at their posts, the ammunition piled ready for use, the groups of civilian spectators standing nearby, the evening stillness. Then the dull resonance of the shots the Martians fired and the clumsy projectile whirling over and smashing on the ground.

Imagine the swiftly spreading coils and tendrils of that blackness towering up toward the heavens, turning the twilight to darkness, a strange and horrible vapor creeping among its victims. Men and horses running, shrieking, falling. Shouts of dismay, the guns suddenly abandoned, men choking and writhing on the ground, and the swift broadening-out of the opaque dome of smoke. And then night and extinction—nothing but a silent mass of thick vapor hiding its dead.

Dawn found the black smoke pouring through the southern suburbs as the government, in its last dying gasp, notified the population that they must flee to the north.

**CHAPTER 15**

# The Exodus from London

**THINK** about the roaring wave of fear that swept through the greatest city in the world just as Monday was dawning. The stream of people in flight, rising quickly into a torrent, lashing in a foaming tumult around the railway stations, got all dammed up into a horrible struggle at the shipping docks on the river Thames. They were fleeing in panic by every available channel northward and eastward. By ten o'clock, the police were losing control and the mass of humanity was running wild.

All the railway lines north of the Thames had been warned about the exodus by midnight on Sunday and to expect tremendous crowds. People were fighting savagely for standing-room in the carriages. Later, people were being trampled and crushed a couple of hundred yards or more from Liverpool Street Station. Revolvers were fired, people stabbed, and the policemen who had been sent to direct the traffic, exhausted and infuriated, were breaking the heads of the people they were called out to protect.

And as the day advanced, and the train engineers and helpers refused to return to London, the pressure of the flight drove the people in an ever-thickening multitude away from the stations and onto the north roads. By midday, a Martian had been seen at the southern city line, and a cloud of slowly-sinking black smoke moved along the Thames and across to the other side, cutting off all escape over the bridges in its sluggish advance.

After a fruitless struggle to get onboard a train in one of the more remote stations he knew about, my brother climbed up on a wall and watched helplessly as the loaded train PLOWED through the shrieking people forced onto the tracks by the mob surrounding the station. He joined the crowd as they ran north in a mad panic. A bicycle shop drew the attention of some of the hysterical crowd, and he joined them as they sacked the store bare. The front tire of the machine he got was damaged, but he got out with no more injury than a cut wrist and proceeded to head north.

He got away from the fury of the panic, and, skirting the larger roads, reached a little town about five miles north of London, tired and hungry. Along the road, people were standing in the roadway, curious, wondering what was going on.

He was passed by a number of cyclists, some horsemen, and two motorcars. A little before he reached the town, his tire went flat, and he abandoned the machine and trudged through the village. There were some shops opened on the main street, and the town people crowded in the doorways and windows, staring at this extraordinary procession of fugitives. He was lucky enough to get some food at an inn before they ran out.

For a time, he remained in the town not knowing what to do. The fleeing people increased in number. Many of them, like my brother, seemed inclined to loiter in the place. There was no fresh news of the invaders from Mars.

At that time, the road was crowded, but as yet, far from congested. Most of the fugitives at that hour were mounted on bicycles, but there were soon motorcars, hansom cabs, and carriages hurrying along, and the dust hung in heavy clouds along the road.

Attempting to go east where some friends of his lived, my brother went along a quiet lane running in that direction. He saw few fugitives until he happened upon two ladies who became his fellow travelers. He came upon them just in time to save them.

He heard their screams, and, hurrying around the corner, saw a couple of men struggling to drag them out of the little pony-cart they had been driving, while a third scoundrel tried to hold the frightened pony's head. One of the ladies, a short woman dressed in white, was simply screaming. The other, a dark, slender figure, slashed her whip at the man attacking her.

My brother immediately grasped the situation, shouted, and ran toward the struggle. One of the men broke away and turned to face him, and my brother, being an expert boxer, went at him right off and knocked him down against the wheel of the cart bleeding from his nose and mouth.

It was no time for boxing chivalry, and my brother laid him out cold with a kick into his damaged face. He then grabbed the collar of the man who held the slender lady's arm. The third antagonist snuck up and struck him from behind, and the man he held wrenched himself free and ran off.

Partly stunned, my brother found himself facing the man who had been holding the horse. He saw the cart taking off down the lane with both of the women staring back at him. The burly roughneck tried to close in, and my brother stopped him with a blow in the face. Then, realizing that he was deserted, he dodged around and tore off down the lane after the cart, with one enemy close behind him and the other following a bit more slowly.

Suddenly, he stumbled and fell; his immediate pursuer tripped over him and went to the ground, and he rose to his feet to find himself facing the two ruffians. He would have had little chance against them, but the slender lady stopped and ran back to help. It seems she had had a revolver all this time, but it had been under the seat when she and her companion were first attacked. She fired at six yards' distance, narrowly missing my brother. The less courageous of the robbers screamed and ran off, and his companion followed him, cursing his cowardice. They both stopped down the lane, where the third man still lay insensible.

"Take this!" said the slender lady, and she gave my brother her revolver.

"Let's go back to the cart," wheezed my brother, wiping the blood from his split lip.

She turned without a word—they were both panting—and they ran back to where the lady in white struggled to hold the frightened pony.

The robbers had had enough. When my brother looked again, they were retreating.

"I'll sit here, if I may," said my brother as he got up on the empty front seat. The slender lady got up beside him, and the lady in white climbed into the rear of the cart. The slender lady said, "Give me the reins," and laid the whip along the pony's side. In another moment, a bend in the road hid the three robbers from my brother's eyes.

So, to his surprise, my brother found himself, panting, with a cut mouth, a bruised jaw, and bloodstained knuckles, driving along with these two women. He learned they were the wife and the younger sister of a surgeon living nearby. The man had heard the news of the Martian advance and had hurried home to help the women escape. He packed some provisions, put his revolver under the seat—luckily for my brother—and told them to drive east. He stayed behind to warn the neighbors and said he would catch up with them early in the morning after gathering some first aid supplies at the hospital. It was nearly nine, and they had seen nothing of him.

My brother promised to stay with them, at least until they could determine what to do, or until the missing man arrived. He let them believe he was an expert shot with the revolver—a weapon strange to him—in order to give them confidence.

Later, they made camp by the side of the road. He told them of his escape out of London, and all that he knew about the Martians. After awhile, their talk died out and gave way to an uneasy state of anticipation. Several refugees came along the lane, and the ladies asked for news. Every answer they got deepened their concept of the disaster that had hit humanity. It also made my brother more anxious to continue their flight. He spoke again of the need to start moving.

"We have money," said the slender woman, and hesitated as she looked at him.

"So have I," said my brother finishing her thought.

She explained that they had as much as thirty pounds in gold, plus some paper money, and suggested that with that they might get on a train at one of the bigger towns ahead. My brother told her about the insanity of the city people as they tried to get onto the trains, and he explained his idea of traveling to a seaport and escaping from the country altogether.

The married lady—the woman in white— would listen to no reasoning, and insisted that they must meet up with her husband; but her sister-in-law was astonishingly quiet and deliberate, and at last agreed to my brother's suggestion. So, planning to cross the Great North Road, they went toward the east.

They began to meet more people on the narrow lane. For the most part these folks were haggard and dirty and were walking with staring eyes and murmuring voices. My brother noticed a pale haze rising among the houses in front of them, and the ladies suddenly cried out as they saw tongues of smoky red flame leaping up. The tumultuous noise they had been hearing resolved itself into the disorderly mingling of voices, the grinding of many wheels, the creaking of wagons, and the staccato of hoofs. Their quiet lane joined up with the main road in another fifty yards, and they could not believe their eyes.

"Good heavens!" cried the lady in white. "What is this you are driving us into?"

The main road was a boiling stream of people, a torrent of human beings moving northward. A great cloud of dust, white and luminous in the blaze of the sun, made everything within twenty feet of the ground gray and indistinct. The dust cloud was stirred up by a dense crowd of horses and men and women, and by the wheels of vehicles of every description, crammed together in a river of humanity.

"Make way!" my brother heard voices crying. "Make way!"

It was like riding into the smoke of a fire to approach the meeting point of the lane and road. The crowd roared like a fire, and the dust was hot and foul smelling. And, indeed, a little way up the road, a villa was burning and sending rolling masses of dense smoke across the road to add to the confusion.

As much as they could see of the road to the right was a tumultuous stream of dirty, hurrying people, crowded in between the villas on either side. The black heads and the crowded forms grew clear as they rushed toward the corner, hurried past, and merged their individuality again in a receding multitude that was swallowed up at last in a cloud of dust.

"Go on! Go on!" cried the voices. "Make way! Get out of the way!"

The previous towns they passed had been scenes of confusion, one was a riotous tumult, but this was a whole population in movement. It is hard to imagine that crowd of people. It had no character of its own. The figures poured out past the corner, and receded with their backs to the group in the lane. Along the margin came those who were on foot and threatened by the wheels of carts and carriages and wagons, stumbling in the ditches, blundering into one another.

The vehicles crowded close to one another, making little way for those swifter and more impatient vehicles that darted forward every now and then when an opportunity showed itself, sending the people scattering against the fences and gates of the villas.

"Push on!" was the cry. "Hurry up! They are coming!"

There were cabs, carriages, shop cars, wagons beyond counting; a mail cart, a road-cleaner's cart, a huge timber wagon crowded with rough necks. A brewer's tanker rumbled by with its wheels splashed with fresh blood.

"Clear the way!" cried the voices. "Clear the way!"

There were sad, haggard women tramping by, some were well dressed, with children that cried and stumbled, their dainty clothes smothered in dust, their weary faces smeared with tears. With many of these came men, sometimes helpful, sometimes frowning and savage. Fighting side by side with them pushed some weary street outcasts in faded rags, wide-eyed, loud-voiced, and foul-mouthed. There were sturdy workmen thrusting their way along and men clothed like clerks or shopkeepers, struggling spasmodically. My brother noticed a wounded soldier and men dressed in the clothes of railway porters. He even saw one wretched creature in a nightshirt with a coat thrown over it.

But varied as it was, the crowd had certain things in common. There was fear and pain on their faces, and fear behind them. A commotion up the road, a quarrel for space between two wagons, sent the whole mass of the crowd quickening their pace for a moment. The heat and dust had been at work on this multitude. Their skins were dry, their lips black and cracked. They all seemed to be thirsty, weary, and footsore. And amid the various cries one heard disputes, groans of weariness and fatigue; the voices of most of them were hoarse and weak. Through it all ran a refrain:

"Make way! Make way! The Martians are coming!"

Few stopped and came aside from that flood. The lane joined the main road at a narrow opening and had a false appearance of coming from the direction of London. Yet a kind of eddy of people moved into our little path. They were weaklings elbowed out of the stream, who for the most part stopped and rested only a moment before plunging back into it again. A little way down the lane, with two friends bending over him, lay a man with a bare leg wrapped with bloody rags. He was a lucky man to have friends.

A little old man, with a gray military moustache and a filthy black frock coat, limped out and sat down close to us, removed his boot—his sock was blood-stained—shook out a pebble, and hobbled on again.

"They are coming," said a man on horseback, riding past along the lane.

"Out of the way, there!" bawled a coachman, towering high; and my brother saw a closed carriage turning into the lane.

The people crushed back on one another to avoid the horse and the wheels of the carriage. My brother pushed the pony and cart back into the hedge, and the man drove by and stopped at the turn. It was a carriage set up for a pair of horses, but only one was in the harness. My brother saw through the dust that two men lifted out a white stretcher and put it gently on the grass.

One of the men came running to my brother.

"Where is there any water?" he asked. "He is dying fast and is very thirsty. It is Lord Garrick."

"Lord Garrick!" exclaimed my brother. "The Chief Justice?"

"The water?" he asked again.

"Look over by the houses! There may be a faucet still working in one of the houses. We have no water. I dare not leave my people."

The man pushed against the crowd toward the gate of the corner house.

"Get away!" said the people, shoving him back. "They are coming! Get out of the way!"

He saw one of his ladies covering her eyes in horror, and shouted, "We must go back!" and began turning the pony round. "We cannot cross this—hell," and he led them back a hundred yards the way they had come, until the fighting crowd was hidden. The two women sat silent, crouching in the cart and shivering.

Then beyond the bend my brother stopped again. The young woman was white and pale, and her sister-in-law sat weeping, too wretched even to call upon her missing husband. My brother was horrified. As soon as they retreated he realized how urgent and unavoidable it was to return again and attempt getting on the main road. He turned to the younger woman, suddenly resolute.

"We must go that way," he said, pointing back toward the horrible road, and led the pony around again.

For the second time that day, the pretty girl proved her quality. To force their way into the torrent of people, my brother plunged into the traffic and slowed down a horse-drawn cab, while she drove the pony in front of it. A wagon locked wheels for a moment and ripped a long scratch along the side of the cart. In another moment, they were caught up and swept forward by the stream. My brother, with the cabman's whip marks red across his face and hands, scrambled into the cart and took the reins.

"Point the revolver at the man behind us," he said, giving it to her, "if he presses us too hard, shoot the . . . No! Point the gun at his horse!"

Then he began to look for a chance of edging to the right across the road. But once in the stream, he seemed to lose any control and became a part of that dusty rout. They swept through the next town with the torrent and were nearly a mile beyond it before they fought across to the opposite side of the way. It was din and confusion; but beyond the town the road split repeatedly, and this relieved some of the stress and congestion as parts of the crowd went their separate ways.

They struck eastward, and soon came upon a great multitude of people drinking at a stream, some fighting to get at the water. And farther on, they saw two trains running slowly, one after the other—trains swarming with people, with men even in the coal bins behind the engines—going northward along the Great Northern Railway.

My brother thought they must have loaded up with passengers outside London, for he had experienced the furious terror there himself and did not think anyone could get out of the city.

They pulled over on a side path and halted for the rest of the afternoon. The violence of the day had exhausted all three of them. They began to suffer the beginnings of hunger; the night turned cold, and none of them dared to sleep. Many people came hurrying along the path near their stopping place, fleeing from unknown dangers, some even going back toward London.

**CHAPTER 16**

# The *Thunder Child*

**HAD** the Martians aimed only at destruction, they could have annihilated the entire population of London on Monday. Not only along the roads to the north and east, but also south from the Thames to the west poured the same frantic rout. If one could have hung in a balloon above London, every northward and eastward road running out of the tangled maze of streets would have seemed covered with the streaming fugitives—a human agony of terror and physical distress.

I have set forth at length in the last chapter, my brother's account of the roads he took, so the reader may realize how that swarming humanity appeared to one who was in their midst. Never before in the history of the world had such a mass of human beings moved and suffered together. The legendary hosts of Goths and Huns, the largest armies Asia has ever seen, would have been but a drop in that current. And this was no disciplined march; it was a stampede—a giant and terrible stampede—without order and without a goal, six million people with no provisions, running away from the city. It was the beginning of the rout of civilization, of the massacre of mankind.

Directly below him, the balloonist would have seen the network of streets far and wide, houses, churches, squares, gardens—already derelict—spread out like a huge map, and in the south the area looked BLOTTED OUT. To the south, it would have seemed as if some monstrous pen had flung ink on the map. Steadily, incessantly, each black splash grew and spread, shooting out this way and that, now banking itself against rising ground, now pouring swiftly over a crest into a new-found valley, exactly like a blob of ink would spread itself out on blotting paper.

And beyond, over the blue hills that rise south of the river, the Martians went to and fro, calmly and methodically spreading their poison cloud over this patch of country and then over that one. They do not seem to have aimed at extermination so much as at complete demoralization and the destruction of any opposition.

The Martians blew up any stockpiles of gunpowder they found, cut every telegraph, and wrecked the railways here and there. They were damaging mankind any way they could. They seemed in no hurry to extend the area of their operations and did not go beyond the central part of London all that day. Many people in London might have stayed in their houses through Monday morning.

Until about midday, the Port of London was an astonishing scene. Steamboats and shipping of all sorts gathered there, tempted by the enormous sums of money offered by people trying to escape the city. About one o'clock in the afternoon, the thinning remnant of a cloud of the black smoke appeared flowing down under one of the main bridges. The Port instantly became a scene of mad confusion, fighting, and collision. Many of the boats got jammed together under the northern arch of the Tower Bridge. The sailors had to fight against the people who swarmed up to them from the riverfront. People were actually clambering down the piers of the bridge from above. An hour later a Martian appeared at the Clock Tower and waded down the river, now filled with nothing but floating wreckage.

I will tell you about the fifth cylinder soon, but first the story of the sixth shell. The sixth star fell to the east. My brother, keeping watch beside the women as they rested in a meadow, saw its green flash far beyond the hills. On Tuesday the little party, still attempting to escape by sea, made its way toward the nearest port. The news that the Martians were now in possession of London was confirmed. They had been seen in the northern suburbs and even a few miles north of the city line.

After only a short time on the run, the scattered multitudes began to realize their need for food. As the mobs grew hungry, the property rights of others ceased to exist. Farmers went out to defend their cattle, granaries, and ripening crops with firearms in their hands. A number of people, like my brother, were traveling eastward, and there were some desperate souls even going back toward London to get food. These were mainly people from the northern suburbs, whose knowledge of the black smoke came by hearsay. He heard that about half the government had gathered in a city twenty miles north, and that enormous quantities of high explosive mines were being buried just north of London.

He was also told that railway service had resumed and trains were running northward to relieve the congestion of the southern counties. There was a rumor that large stores of flour were available in the northern towns and that within twenty-four hours bread would be distributed among the starving people scattered to the north of London. But this intelligence did not alter his plan of escape, and the three refugees went east all day and heard no more about bread distribution or any other false promises. Nor, as a matter of fact, did anyone else hear anymore about it. That night they saw the falling of the seventh star.

On Wednesday they reached a nasty little

town where a group of the inhabitants, calling themselves the Committee of Public Supply, seized the pony. All my brother and his ladies got for their dependable beast was the promise of a share of its meat the next day.

People were watching for Martians from the church towers. My brother wanted to push on to the coast at once rather than wait for their portion of the meat, although all three of them were very hungry. By midday, they came in sight of the sea, and saw the most amazing assembly of shipping ever gathered together in one place.

After the ships could no longer come up the river Thames, they came over to the east coast to pick up passengers. They lay in a huge sickle-shaped curve that vanished into mist at last toward the North. Close inshore, it seemed like there were a thousand smaller boats—English, Scotch, French, Dutch, and Swedish; steam launches from the Thames, yachts, and even electric boats. Out to sea were the larger ships—several coal haulers, trim merchantmen, cattle ships, passenger boats, petroleum tankers, and tramp steamers.

A couple of miles out cruised an ironclad warship, very low in the water. It was the only warship in sight, but far away to the southeast could be seen the smoke marking more of the fleet's warships. These ships maneuvered in an extended line, steam up and ready for action against the Martian invaders, vigilant and yet powerless to stop them.

At the sight of the sea, the married lady, in spite of the assurances of her sister-in-law, started to panic. She had never been out of England before, she would rather die than escape to a foreign country, and so forth. She seemed, poor woman, to imagine that the French and the Martians might prove to be very similar. She had been growing increasingly hysterical, fearful, and depressed during their journey. Her wish was to return to her home—she was positive they would find her husband at home.

They finally got her down to the beach, where my brother succeeded in attracting the attention of some men on a paddle steamer. The men said the steamer was going to France. After paying the fare, they found themselves safely aboard the steamboat. There was food available on the boat, though at exorbitant prices.

There were already thirty or so passengers onboard, some of whom had spent the last of their money in securing a passage. The captain stayed in place until late in the afternoon, picking up passengers until the decks were dangerously crowded. He probably would have stayed longer if not for the sound of cannon fire from the south. The warship patrolling nearby suddenly fired a small gun and hoisted a string of flags. A jet of smoke poured out of her funnels as she prepared to steam away.

The passengers noticed that the firing was growing louder. At the same time, in the southeast, three warships came in view far out to sea beneath clouds of smoke. But my brother's attention was drawn to the south where he heard distant firing and saw flames rising out of the distant gray haze.

The little steamer was already making her way toward the east, and the coast was growing blue and hazy as we pulled away. A Martian appeared, small and faint in the remote distance, moving up from the south. Spotting the monster, the captain swore at the top of his voice, and the ship seemed infected with his terror. Every soul aboard stood at the rail or up on the seats and stared at that distant shape, higher than the trees or church towers, as it advanced with the leisurely parody of a human stride.

It was the first Martian my brother had seen, and he stood, more amazed than terrified, watching this Titan advancing deliberately toward the ships in the channel, wading farther and farther out into the water. Then, a few miles to the south, came another Martian, striding over some stunted trees, and then yet another, still farther off, wading through a shiny mudflat near the shore. They were all moving seaward, as if to intercept the escape of the many vessels that were crowded in close to the shore. In spite of our little paddleboat's noisy engines, and the white-foam flung behind her, she moved away from this ominous advance with terrifying slowness.

Glancing to the north, my brother saw the large group of ships already writhing around in panic at the approaching terror; one ship passing another, another changing direction to take advantage of a clearing in the massed confusion, steamships whistling and giving off volumes of smoke, sails being let out, launches rushing hither and thither. He was so fascinated by this and by the approaching danger away to the left that he had no eyes for anything seaward. And then a swift movement of the steamboat (she had suddenly turned to avoid being run down) made him fall off the chair he was standing on. There was shouting all around him, a trampling of feet, and a cheer that seemed to be answered faintly.

He jumped to his feet and saw off to the side, not a hundred yards away, a vast iron bulk tearing through the water like the blade of a plow, tossing water on either side in huge waves of foam that leaped toward the steamer, flinging her paddles helplessly in the air, and then sucking her deck down almost to the surface of the water.

Spray blinded my brother for a moment. When his eyes were clear again, he saw the warship had passed by and was rushing toward land. Her superstructure rose out of the sleek hull, and from that, twin funnels stood at a rakish angle and spat up a smoking blast shot through with fire. It was the destroyer, *Thunder Child,* steaming at full throttle, coming to the rescue of the threatened shipping.

Keeping his footing on the heaving deck by clutching the railing, my brother looked past this charging warship at the Martians again. He saw the three of them now close together, and standing so far out to sea that their tripod supports were almost entirely submerged. Seen in that remote perspective, they appeared far less formidable than the huge iron bulk in whose wake the steamer was pitching so helplessly.

It seemed like they were regarding this new antagonist with astonishment. The *Thunder Child* did not fire, but simply charged them at full speed. It was probably her not firing that enabled her to get so near the enemy. The Martians did not know what to make of her. If she had fired one shell, they would have instantly sent her to the bottom with their Heat Ray.

She was steaming at such a pace that in a minute she seemed halfway between the steamboat and the Martians—a diminishing dark bulk against the receding expanse of the coast.

Suddenly, the front Martian lowered his tube and discharged a canister of the black gas at the warship. It hit her side and bounced off and then emitted a torrent of black smoke, from which the warship moved clear. To the watchers on the steamer, low in the water and with the sun in their eyes, it seemed as though she were already among the Martians.

They saw the Martians separating and rising out of the water as they retreated shoreward, and one of them raised his Heat Ray. He held it pointing downward, and an eruption of steam sprang from the water close to the destroyer. It must have driven through the ship's side like a white-hot iron rod through paper.

A flicker of flame went up through the rising steam, and then the Martian reeled and staggered. In another moment, he was cut down, and a great body of water and steam shot high in the air. The guns of the *Thunder Child* sounded through the chaos, going off one after the other. One shot splashed the water close by the steamer, ricocheted toward the other fleeing ships to the north, and smashed a large fishing boat to matchwood.

But no one paid much attention. At the sight of the Martian's collapse, the captain on the bridge yelled out, and all the passengers on the steamer's stern shouted together. And then they yelled again. For, surging out beyond the white tumult, raced something long and black, flames streaming from its middle parts and its ventilators and funnels spouting fire.

She was still alive, the steering gear was intact and her engines working. She headed straight for a second Martian, and was within a hundred yards of him when the Heat Ray came to bear. Then, with a violent thud and a blinding flash, her decks, her funnels, the entire top of the ship, leaped upward. The Martian staggered with the violence of her explosion, and in another moment, the flaming wreckage, still driving forward, struck him and crumpled him up like a thing of cardboard. My brother shouted involuntarily. A boiling tumult of steam hid everything again.

"Two down!" yelled the captain.

Everyone was shouting. The whole steamer, from end to end, rang with frantic cheering that was taken up, first by one, and then by all of the ships and boats racing out to sea.

The steam hung over the water for many minutes, hiding the third Martian and the coast altogether. And all this time, my brother's little boat was paddling steadily out to sea and away from the fight. When the confusion cleared, the drifting fog of the Martian's black smoke intervened, and nothing of the *Thunder Child* could be made out, nor could the third Martian be seen. But the warships that had been far out to sea were now quite close and heading in toward shore past the steamboat.

The little vessel continued its way seaward, and the ironclads receded as they steamed toward the coast, which was still hidden by a marbled foggy bank of vapor, part steam and part black smoke, eddying and combining in the strangest way. The fleet of refugees was scattering to the northeast; several boats were sailing between the ironclads and our boat. After a time, and before they reached the dense fog bank, the warships turned northward, and then abruptly turned about and passed into the thickening haze of evening. The coast grew faint, and at last was indistinguishable from the low banks of clouds that were gathering around the sinking sun.

Then suddenly, out of the golden haze of the sunset came the booming of guns, and a form of black shadows moving south. Everyone struggled to the rail of the steamer and peered into the blinding furnace of the west, but nothing could be seen clearly. A mass of smoke rose and barred the face of the sun. Our little steamboat throbbed on its way.

The sun sank into the clouds, the sky flushed and darkened, and the evening star trembled into sight. It was deep twilight when the captain cried out and pointed. My brother strained his eyes. Something flew up into the sky out of the grayness—rushed upward into the clearness above the clouds in the western sky; something flat and broad, and very large. It swept around in a wide curve, grew smaller, sank slowly, and vanished again into the gray mystery of the night. And as it flew it rained down a cloud of darkness on the land.

# BOOK TWO

# THE EARTH UNDER THE MARTIANS

**CHAPTER 1**

# Under Foot

**IN** the first book, I strayed from my adventures to tell you about my brother's experiences with the two ladies. I will now resume my story. The priest and I stopped and hid Sunday night and all the next day—the day of the panic—in a little island of daylight, cut off by the black smoke from the rest of the world. We could do nothing but wait during those two weary days.

Needless to say, I was extremely anxious about my wife. I imagined that she was still in Smithville, terrified, in danger, and worrying about me. I paced the rooms and cried out loud when I thought of how I was cut off from her and of all that might happen to her with me not around. I knew my cousin was brave enough for most emergencies, but he was not the sort of man to understand danger quickly or to take initiative. My only consolation was to believe that the Martians were moving north toward London and away from her.

I grew weary of the priest's constant complaints and selfish despair. After a while, I went upstairs in order to be alone with my miseries. There were signs of other people in a neighboring house on Sunday evening—a face at a window and moving lights, and later the slamming of a door. But I do not know who these people were, nor what became of them. We saw nothing in that house the next day. The black smoke drifted slowly over to the river, creeping nearer and nearer, seeping along the roadway outside the house.

A Martian fighting machine came across the fields about midday, with some new kind of weapon that shot a jet of superheated steam that hissed against the walls, smashed all the windows it touched, and scalded the priest's hand as he fled out of the front room. We both hid in the basement, and when we looked outside again, the country looked like a black snowstorm had passed over. Looking toward the river, we were astonished to see red-colored plants mixed in with the black of the scorched meadows.

Since the black smoke had dissipated and turned to dust, I saw that we were no longer trapped and could get away. But now that we could take some action, the priest was lethargic and unreasonable.

"We are safe here," he repeated; "safe here, safe here."

I decided to just let him stay where he was and enjoy his misery. Since I was wiser now, thanks to the soldier's teaching, I scrounged up some food and water. I also found oil and rags for my burns, and took a hat and a flannel shirt that I found in one of the bedrooms. When it was clear that I meant to go on alone, he suddenly got up and wanted to follow me. We started out along the blackened road going north.

All along the road, we found the dead bodies of horses and people lying in contorted positions, along with overturned carts and luggage. Everything was covered with the black dust. We got a few miles without any problems and then found a patch of green. We went through this park-like setting, with its deer going to and fro under the trees, and even saw some men and women hurrying north in the distance. These were the first live people we saw.

Across the road, the woods to the south were still on fire. The town we were walking through had escaped both the Heat Ray and black smoke, and there were more people around here, though none could give us any news. For the most part, they were like we were, taking advantage of a lull in the action to move someplace else. I thought many of the houses here were still occupied by their owners who were too frightened to run away.

We crossed over a broad stream about half past eight. We quickly ran across the exposed bridge, of course, but I noticed several red masses floating beneath us, some many feet across. I did not have time to look at them, but I knew I had never seen anything like them before. On the other side, we again saw the black dust that had once been the black smoke, and dead bodies—a heap near the train station; but we did not see any Martians until we were almost out of the little town.

Then suddenly, we saw people running and the upper part of a Martian fighting machine appeared over some housetops, not a hundred yards away! We stood frozen in shock, and if the Martian had looked down, we would have been killed. We were so terrified that we could hardly move, but finally turned aside and hid in a shed. The priest crouched down in a corner, weeping silently, and refused to move.

But my goal of reaching my wife in Smithville would not let me rest, and in the twilight I went out again. I made my way to the north road. I thought I left the priest in the shed, but he came after me.

That second attempt to go to my wife was a foolhardy thing to do, since it was obvious that the Martians were all around us. No sooner had the priest caught up with me than we saw another Martian across the meadows in the direction we were going. Four or five shadowy figures ran in front of it across the field, and in a moment, it was plain that the Martian was chasing them. In three strides he was among them, and they scattered in all directions. He did not use his Heat Ray to destroy them, but instead picked them up one by one and tossed them into a large metallic carrier attached behind him.

It was the first time I realized that the Martians might have another purpose for humanity other than its complete destruction. We stood there petrified for a moment, then turned and fled through a field, fell into a ditch, and lay there, not even daring to whisper.

I suppose it was nearly eleven o'clock before we found enough courage to get up and get going again. We no longer traveled on the road, but snuck along hedgerows and through fields. We watched through the gloom, he on the right and I on the left, for the Martians, who seemed to be all around us. In one place we came upon a scorched and blackened area, now cooling and ashen, and a bunch of dead bodies. They were horribly burned about their heads and trunks, but their legs and boots were mostly intact. They were fifty feet behind a line of four melted cannons and smashed gun carriages.

The next town seemed to have escaped destruction, but the place was silent and deserted. We did not see any dead people, though the night was too dark for us to see much of anything. My companion suddenly complained of hunger and thirst, and we decided to try to break into one of the houses.

The first house we entered was small and already looted, and we found nothing edible left in the place but some moldy cheese. I did find some water, and I also took a hatchet, which might prove useful in our next housebreaking.

We crossed the road to a white house inside a walled garden, and found some food—two loaves of bread, an uncooked steak, and half of a ham. We also found several bottles of beer, a sack of beans, and a dozen or so cans of soup, salmon and vegetables.

We sat in the kitchen in the dark—not daring to strike a light—and ate bread and ham, and drank beer out of the same bottle. The priest wanted to keep going instead of resting and eating. I was urging him to eat and keep up his strength when, all of a sudden, disaster struck!

"It can't be midnight yet," I was saying, and then came a blinding glare of green light! Everything in the kitchen leaped out, clearly visible in green and black, and vanished again. This was followed by a roar, like the explosion of the biggest bomb in the world! Then came the clash of breaking glass, a crash and rattle of falling masonry all around us, and the plaster of the ceiling came down, smashing onto our heads. I was knocked out cold, and when I came to we were in darkness again.

For a little while, I could not figure out what had happened. Then things started to come back to me.

"Are you all right?" asked the priest in a whisper.

"Don't move," he added, "the floor is covered with smashed plates and glass from the cabinets. You can't possibly move without making a noise, and THEY are outside!"

We both sat silently and could almost hear each other breathing. Everything seemed deadly still, but something near us, some plaster or broken brickwork, slid down with a rumbling sound. Outside and very near was an intermittent, metallic rattle.

"What was that?" squeaked the priest when it happened again.

"Yes," I said. "What happened?"

"A Martian!" whispered the priest.

"It did not sound like the Heat Ray," I said softly, and thought that one of their fighting machines had stumbled against the house like I had seen one stumble against a building before.

Our situation was so strange that for hours and hours we scarcely moved. Finally the morning light filtered in, not through the window, which remained black, but through a hole in the wall behind us.

Outside, the soil appeared to be banked up high against the house. At the top of the window frame we could see an uprooted drainpipe. The floor was littered with smashed glassware; the end of the kitchen toward the house was separated from the wall and since the daylight seemed to be coming in there, we thought the rest of the house had collapsed.

As the day grew brighter, we saw through the gap in the wall the body of a tripod Martian fighting machine, standing guard over the still glowing cylinder that apparently had just landed. At the sight of that, we crawled out of the light of the kitchen and into the darkness of the basement.

I suddenly figured out what was going on and whispered, "The fifth cylinder! It was the fifth shot from Mars that has struck this house and buried us under the ruins!"

For a time the priest was silent, and then whispered, "God have mercy upon us!"

We stayed perfectly still in the basement; I hardly dared to breathe, and sat with my eyes fixed on the dim light from the door at the top of the stairs. When I shifted my gaze I could just see the priest's face, a dim, oval shape, and his collar and cuffs. Outside a metallic hammering started up, then a loud hooting, and after a quiet interval, a hissing sound like a steam engine. These noises continued and seemed to increase in volume as time wore on. After a while, a pounding noise started, followed by a vibration that made everything around us shake. Once the light was blocked out, and the ghostly kitchen doorway became absolutely dark. We stayed there for many hours, silent and shivering, until we collapsed into fitful sleep.

I woke up and found myself very hungry. My hunger was so insistent that it moved me to action. I told the priest I was going to look for food and quietly made my way up to the kitchen. He did not answer, but as soon as I began eating, I heard him crawling toward me.

**CHAPTER 2**

# What We Saw from the Ruined House

**AFTER** eating, we crept back to the basement, and I must have dozed off again. When I opened my eyes, I found that I was alone. The thudding vibration continued with wearisome persistence. I whispered for the priest several times, and at last felt my way up the stairs to the door of the kitchen. It was still daylight, and I saw him across the room, looking out at the Martians. His shoulders were hunched, and his head was hidden from me.

I could hear a number of noises like in a locomotive repair shop, and the place rocked with that beating thud. Through the hole in the wall, I could see the top of a tree touched with golden sunlight and the warm blue of a tranquil evening sky. For a minute or so I remained watching the man, and then I approached him, crouching and stepping with extreme care amid the broken stuff that littered the floor.

I touched his leg, and he jumped so violently that a mass of plaster went sliding down outside and fell with a loud noise. I gripped his arm, fearing he might cry out, and for a long time we froze motionless. The falling plaster left a vertical slit open in the debris, and by raising myself across a beam, I was able to see out of this gap into what had been a quiet suburban roadway.

The fifth cylinder must have fallen right into the house we had first visited. The building had vanished, completely smashed and blown apart by the blow. The cylinder lay far beneath the original foundation—deep in a hole. The earth all round it had splashed up under that tremendous impact—"splashed" is the only word —and lay in heaped piles that hid the adjacent houses. Our house had collapsed backward; the front portion had been destroyed completely; by chance the kitchen and part of the basement had escaped, and stood buried now under soil and ruins, closed in by tons of earth on every side except toward the cylinder. We hung on the very edge of the circular pit where the Martians were now working. The heavy beating sound was close by, and occasionally, a bright green vapor rose up like a veil across our peephole.

The cylinder was already opened, and on the farther edge, amid the smashed and gravel-heaped shrubbery, one of the great fighting machines, deserted by its occupant, stood stiff and tall against the evening sky. At first, I hardly noticed the pit and the cylinder, although it has been convenient to describe them first. What really caught my eye was the extraordinary machine I saw scuttling around inside the pit and the hideous creatures that were crawling slowly and painfully near it.

It was the machine that first caught my attention. It looked like a metallic spider with five jointed, agile legs, and with an extraordinary number of jointed levers, bars, and clutching tentacles around its body. Most of its arms were retracted, but with three long tentacles, it was fishing out a number of rods, plates, and bars from inside the cylinder.

The machine's motion was so swift, complex, and perfect that at first I did not see it as a machine, in spite of its metallic glitter. The tall fighting machines were animated to an extraordinary degree, but they were nothing compared with this. People who have never seen this piece of machinery, but have only seen photographs or heard the imperfect descriptions of such eye-witnesses as myself, could not comprehend their appearance of almost being alive.

At first the spider-like thing did not seem like a machine, but instead appeared to be a crablike creature with a glittering metallic outside skin. The Martian, whose delicate tentacles controlled its movements, looked to be simply the equivalent of the crab's brain. But then I saw the resemblance of the "brain's" gray-brown, shiny, leathery skin to that of the other sprawling bodies gathered around this shiny machine, and the true nature of this incredible workman dawned upon me. With the realization that this was a machine controlled by a living Martian, my interest shifted to those other creatures, the real Martians. I had already had a quick view of them, and my initial revulsion no longer obscured my observation.

They were, I now saw, the most unearthly creatures it is possible to imagine. They had huge round bodies—or, rather, heads—about four feet in diameter, each body having a face in front. This face had no nostrils—indeed, the Martians do not seem to have had any sense of smell, but it had a pair of very large dark-colored eyes, and just beneath the eyes was a kind of fleshy beak. In the back of this head or body—I scarcely know how to describe it—was a single, tight, drum-like surface. We later learned that this was anatomically an ear, though it must have been almost useless in our dense atmosphere. In a group around the mouth were sixteen slender, almost whip-like tentacles, arranged in two bunches of eight each. When I saw the Martians for the first time, they seemed to be attempting to raise themselves up on these tentacles, but of course, with the increased weight of earthly gravity, this was impossible. I guess on Mars they may have used them as a means of locomotion.

Their internal anatomy, as dissection has since shown, was almost equally simple. The greater part of the structure was the brain, sending enormous nerves to the eyes, ear, and tentacles. Under the brain were two bulky lungs connected to the mouth, and, finally, the heart and its vessels. The distress on their heart and lungs, caused by our denser atmosphere and greater gravitational attraction, seemed to cause the convulsive movements of their outer skin.

And this was the sum of the Martian organs. Strange as it may seem to a human being, all the complex apparatus of digestion, which makes up the bulk of our bodies, did not exist in the Martians. They were heads—merely heads. They did not have any entrails. They did not eat, much less digest. Instead, they took the fresh, living blood of other creatures, and INJECTED it into their own veins. I have seen this being done, as I shall mention later. Let it be enough to say that blood, obtained from a still living animal, in most cases from a human being, was sucked by means of a little pipette into the recipient's. . . .

The idea of this is no doubt horribly repulsive to us, but at the same time I think that we should remember how repulsive our carnivorous habits would seem to an intelligent rabbit.

The physiological advantages of this Martian

technique of injection of nutrients are undeniable, if one thinks of the tremendous waste of human time and energy devoted to eating and the digestive process. One half of our bodies are made up of glands and tubes and organs, occupied in turning food into nutrients for our blood. The digestive processes and their reaction on the nervous system sap our strength and affect our minds. Men are happy or miserable depending on if they are hungry or well-fed. They are healthy or unhealthy depending on the state of their livers or gastric glands. But the Martians were lifted above all these organic fluctuations of mood and emotion.

Their undeniable preference for men as their source of nourishment is partly explained by the remains of the victims they had brought with them as provisions from Mars. These creatures, to judge from the remains that have fallen into human hands, were bipeds with flimsy bones and feeble musculature, standing about six feet high and having round, erect heads, and large eyes. Two or three of these seem to have been brought in each cylinder, and all were killed before Earth was reached. It was just as well for them, for the attempt to stand upright on our planet would have broken every bone in their bodies.

In a few other points, the Martian physiology differed strangely from ours. They did not sleep. Since they had no extensive muscular mechanisms to recuperate, the periodical need for rest was unknown to them. They had little or no sense of fatigue, it would seem. On Earth they could never have moved without extreme effort, yet even to the last they kept in action. In twenty-four hours, they did twenty-four hours of work.

In addition, wonderful as it seems in a sexual world, the Martians were absolutely without sex, and therefore, without any of the tumultuous emotions that arise from that difference among men and women.

The last point in which the systems of these creatures differed from ours was in what one might have thought a very trivial matter. Microorganisms, which cause so much disease and pain on Earth, have either never appeared on Mars, or Martian science eliminated them ages ago. The diseases, fevers, and contagions of human life, like the common cold, infections, cancers, tumors and all other such maladies, never enter the life of a Martian.

The Martians appeared to have a hearing organ, a single round drum at the back of the head-body, and eyes with a visual range not very different from ours. It is commonly supposed that they communicated by sounds and gestures with their tentacles. No surviving human saw as much of the Martians in action as I did. I take no credit for that accident, but that is the fact. And

I assert that I watched them closely time after time, and that I have seen four, five, and (once) six of them sluggishly performing the most elaborately complicated operations together without either sound or gesture.

Their peculiar hooting sound always preceded feeding; it had no modulation, and was, I believe, in no sense a signal, but merely the expiration of air in preparation for the suction operation. I am convinced that the Martians interchanged thoughts without any physical means.

We men, with our bicycles, steamships, and our primitive soaring-machines, our guns and electric lights and so forth, are just in the beginning of the evolution that the Martians have almost finished. They have become practically mere brains, wearing different mechanical bodies according to their needs, just as men wear suits of clothes and take a bicycle in a hurry or carry an umbrella in the rain.

While I was still watching their sluggish motions in the sunlight, and noting each strange detail of their form, the priest reminded me of his presence by pulling at my arm. I turned to a scowling face, and silent, eloquent lips. He wanted the viewing slit, only large enough for one of us to peep through at a time; and so I had to stop watching them for a while, so he could enjoy that privilege.

Later, when I looked outside again, the active

spider-machine had already put together several of the pieces it had taken out of the cylinder into another spider-machine. Down on my left, a small digging machine came into view, emitting jets of green vapor and working its way around the pit, digging and moving dirt around in a methodical manner. It was this machine that made the beating noise, along with the rhythmic shocks that kept our demolished house shaking. As far as I could see, the thing operated with no Martian controlling it at all.

## CHAPTER 3

# The Days of Imprisonment

**ANOTHER** fighting machine arrived and drove us from our peephole down into the basement. We were afraid that the Martian might see us hiding behind our barrier as he looked down. Yet, even though it was risky, the attraction of watching them was irresistible. And, as I think back on it now, it is amazing that, in spite of the danger, we would struggle savagely for the privilege of observing the monsters.

The fact is that the priest and I had unbelievably incompatible dispositions. Our habits of thought and action, and the danger and isolation only made the incompatibility worse. I had already come to hate how set in his ways and stupid he was. His endless muttering monologue confounded every effort I made to think. He would weep for hours, and I believe that this spoiled child of life thought his weak tears had an effect on me.

He ate more than I did, and I tried to tell

him that our only chance of survival was to stay inside the house until the Martians finished with their pit activities. I told him that, in time, we might need the food he was consuming at such a rapid rate.

As the days wore on, his lack of consideration made everything so much worse that I had to resort to violence. After a couple of knocks to the head, he would become reasonable for a short time. But he was one of those weak, hateful souls, and he soon returned to his aggravating ways.

And while we carried out our dark, dim contest of whispers, snatched food, and conflict; outside, in the relentless sunlight, was the bizarre activity of the Martians in the pit. After a long time, I ventured back to the peephole to find that the original monsters had been reinforced by three more of the tall, tripod fighting machines. These last had brought fresh contraptions that were now placed around the newly arrived cylinder. The second spider-machine was now completed and was busy working on one of the new contraptions. This new machine had a body resembling a milk can, with a rotating, funnel-shaped receptacle on top. It was generating a stream of gray powder that flowed out onto the ground at its base.

The spider-machine seemed to be servicing the milk-can thing by digging up soil and tossing it into the receptacle. The gray powder flowed out of its base along a channel dug in the earth, which was partially hidden by a mound of blue dust which came out of the side of the device. As I looked, the handling-machine extended a tentacle down to the ground behind the mound. In another second, it had lifted a bar of shiny metal into sight and deposited it in a growing stack of bars that stood at the side of the pit. In just a few hours, this industrious machine must have made more than a hundred such bars, and the mound of bluish dust rose steadily until it was as high as the side of the pit.

The contrast between the quick and complex movements of these machines, and the inert panting clumsiness of their masters was profound, and for days I had to remind myself which of the two were indeed the living things.

The priest was at the viewing slit when the first captured men were brought to the pit. I was watching him from below as he jumped back suddenly. He rushed up beside me in the darkness waving his arms, and for a moment I shared his panic. I got up, stepped across him, and clambered up to the slit. At first, I could see no reason for his frantic behavior. The whole picture was a flickering scene of green flames and shifting black shadows. I could no longer see the Martians, the mound of blue dust hid them from my sight, and a fighting machine was still plainly visible on one side of the pit. And then, amid the noise of the machinery, came the drifting hint of human voices.

I crouched, watching the fighting machine closely, making sure that the hood did indeed contain a Martian. As the green flames shot up, I could see the oily gleam and the brightness of his eyes. Suddenly, I heard terrifying screams, and saw a long tentacle reaching over the shoulder of the fighting machine into the little cage that was attached to its back. Then something—something struggling violently—was lifted high against the sky, a black, vague enigma against the starlight. As this black object came down again, I saw by the green brightness that it was a man. For an instant, he was clearly visible. He was a stout, ruddy, well-dressed middle-aged man. I imagined that three days before he must have been a man of considerable consequence. I could see his staring eyes and open mouth and gleams of light on his studs and watch chain. He vanished behind the mound, and for a moment there was silence. And then I heard him shrieking and a sustained hooting from the Martians.

I slid down to the floor, struggled to my feet, clapped my hands over my ears, and bolted down into the basement. The priest, who had been crouching silently with his arms over his head, looked up as I passed, cried out loudly and came running after me.

That night, as we lurked in the basement, I

tried to think of some plan of escape. Later during the day, I was able to consider our position with greater clearness. The priest was incapable of talking; this new and awful atrocity had robbed him of all vestiges of reason. He had sunk to the level of an animal. It came to me, once I faced the facts, that although we were in great danger, there was no reason for despair. Our main chance was that the Martians were using the pit as nothing more than a temporary encampment. Even if they kept it permanently, they might not consider it necessary to constantly guard it, and we might get a chance to escape.

I also weighed the possibility of digging our way out in a direction away from the pit, but the chances of our emerging within sight of some fighting machine seemed too great. And I knew I would have had to do all the digging myself. The priest was good for nothing this important.

It was on the third day, if my memory serves me right, that I saw the body of the man that had been killed. After that, I avoided the hole in the wall all day. I went down into the basement and spent a few hours digging with my hatchet as silently as possible. When I had made a hole a couple of feet deep, the loose earth collapsed and made a lot of noise, and I did not want to continue. I lost heart, and lay down on the floor for a long time—I did not even have the spirit to move. After that, I abandoned the idea of escaping by digging out of our prison.

The Martians had made such an impression on me that I knew no human effort could help us. But on the fourth or fifth night, I heard a sound like heavy guns. It was very late, and the moon was shining brightly. The Martians had moved the excavating machine out of sight, and, other than a fighting machine at the edge of the pit and a spider-machine that was right below my peephole, the place seemed deserted. Except for the pale glow from the machines and patches of white moonlight, the pit was in darkness and quite still. That night was beautiful; the moon seemed to have the sky all to itself with not a cloud in sight. I heard a dog howling, and that familiar sound made me listen. Then I heard, quite distinctly, a booming exactly like the sound of large guns. I counted six distinct reports, and after a long interval, six again. And that was all.

**CHAPTER 4**

# The Death of the Priest

**IT** was on the sixth day of our imprisonment, as I was looking out our spy hole, that I noticed I was alone. Instead of keeping close to me and trying to shove me away from the viewing slit, the priest had gone back into the basement. I was struck by a sudden thought, and quickly went down to find him. In the darkness, I heard the priest drinking. I reached toward him in the darkness, and my fingers caught his bottle of wine.

For a few minutes, there was a tussle. The bottle struck the floor and broke, and I moved away. We stood panting and threatening each other. In the end, I planted myself between him and the food, and told him that from now on, we had to be disciplined. I divided the food into rations to last us ten days. I would not let him eat any more that day. In the afternoon he made a feeble effort to get at the food. I had been dozing, but in an instant I was awake and stopped him. All day and all night, we sat face to face—I weary but resolute, and he weeping and complaining of his hunger. It was, I know, a night and a day, but to me it seemed an interminable length of time.

And so our incompatibility ended at last in open conflict. For two days, we struggled in undertones and wrestling contests. There were times when I beat and kicked him madly, times when I cajoled and persuaded him, and once I tried to bribe him with the last bottle of wine—I knew I could survive just fine with plain water. But neither force nor kindness worked—he was beyond reason. He would not stop his attacks on the food or stop his babbling to himself. He would not take even the most rudimentary steps to keep our imprisonment endurable. Slowly, I began to realize that he had become unhinged, bonkers, over-the-hill—that my sole companion in this close and sickly darkness was an insane man.

On the eighth day, he began to talk aloud instead of whispering, and nothing I could do would moderate his speech.

"It is just, O God!" he would say, over and over again. "It is just. On me and mine be the punishment laid. We have sinned, we have fallen short. There was poverty, sorrow; the poor were trodden in the dust, and I held my peace. I preached acceptable folly—my God, what folly! —when I should have stood up, though I died for it, and called upon them to repent-repent! . . . Oppressors of the poor and needy . . . ! The wine press of God!"

Then he would suddenly change the subject back to the matter of the food I kept from him, praying, begging, weeping, at last threatening. He began to raise his voice—I begged him to stop. He figured out that he had something on me—he threatened he would shout and bring the Martians down on us. For a time, that scared me; but any concession would have shortened our chance of escape. I defied him, although I felt no assurance that he would not yell out at any time. But that day, at any rate, he did not. He talked with his voice rising slowly, through the greater part of the eighth and ninth days—threatening and begging, mingled with a torrent of half-sane and always rambling, confused repentance for his failure in God's service. Then he slept awhile, and when he woke up, began talking and preaching again with renewed strength, so loudly that I knew I had to make him stop.

"Be still!" I implored.

"I have been still too long," he snapped, in a tone loud enough for the Martians to hear, "and now I must bear my witness. Woe unto this unfaithful city! Woe! Woe! Woe! To the inhabitants of Earth by reason of the other voices of the trumpet . . ."

"Shut up!" I hissed, rising to my feet, terrified that the Martians should hear us. "For God's sake . . ."

"Nay," shouted the priest at the top of his voice, standing and extending his arms. "I! WILL! SPEAK! The word of the Lord is upon me!"

In three strides he was up the stairs and at the door leading into the kitchen.

"I must bear my witness! I go! It has already been too long delayed."

I reached out my hand for the hatchet that was hanging on the wall with some other tools. In a flash I was after him. I was beside myself with fear. Before he was halfway across the kitchen I caught up with him. With one last touch of humanity I turned the blade to the side and struck him with the flat. He went down and lay stretched out on the floor out cold.

Suddenly, I heard a noise outside, and the peephole got dark. I saw the lower surface of a spider-machine moving slowly across the hole. One of its gripping tentacles curled into the room amid the debris; and then another appeared, feeling its way over the fallen beams. I stood there petrified. The machine moved a little bit and I saw, through a sort of glass plate near the edge of the machine's body, the face and large dark eyes of a Martian peering in. Then another long metallic snake of tentacle came slowly through the hole.

I turned, stumbled over the priest, and stopped at the basement door. The tentacle was now some two yards into the room, twisting and turning, with strange sudden movements, this way and that. For a while, I stood and watched, fascinated by that slow, fitful advance. Then, scared out of my wits, I forced myself to quietly creep down the stairs into the basement. I trembled violently; I could barely stand up. I stood there in the darkness staring up at the faintly lit doorway that opened into the kitchen. Had the Martian seen me? What was it doing now?

Something was moving around up there; every now and then it tapped against the wall, or made a faint metallic ringing noise, like the jangling of keys on a ring. Then something heavy— I knew only too well what it was—was dragged across the floor of the kitchen toward the opening to the outside. Unable to resist, I crept back up to the door and looked into the kitchen. Through the peephole, I saw the Martian, inside its spider-machine, scrutinizing the priest's head. I worried that it might figure out my presence from the mark of the blow I had given the priest.

I crept back to the basement and tried to hide behind the coal and firewood in the corner. Every now and then I paused, to hear if the Martian had thrust its tentacles through the opening again.

Then the faint metallic jingle returned. I followed the sound as it slowly made its way all over the kitchen. Presently I heard it nearer—at the doorway leading downstairs. I prayed that its length might be too short to reach me. I prayed copiously. It scraped faintly around the basement door. An age of almost intolerable suspense passed; then I heard it fumbling at the latch. It had found the door! The Martians understood doors!

It worried at the catch for a minute, and then the door opened.

In the darkness, I could barely see the thing—like an elephant's trunk more than anything else—waving toward me and touching and examining the wall, lumps of coal, firewood and ceiling. It was like a worm swaying its blind head to and fro.

Once it touched the heel of my boot. I was on the verge of screaming; I bit my hand. For a time, the tentacle was still and silent. I wondered if it had gone back upstairs. Then, with an abrupt click, it snapped at something—I thought it had me! For a minute, I was not sure. Apparently, it had taken out a lump of coal to examine.

I seized the opportunity of slightly shifting my position, which had become cramped, and then listened. I whispered passionate prayers for safety.

Then I heard the slow, deliberate sound creeping upstairs again. Slowly, slowly it drew up and went through the basement door. I heard it upstairs again, scratching against the walls and moving among the furniture and other debris.

I heard it making more noise in the kitchen, and then it seemed that our hoard of canned goods rattled and a bottle smashed, and there was another heavy bump against the basement door. Then silence that passed into an infinity of suspense.

Had it gone?

I lay all the tenth day in the darkness, buried among coals and firewood, not daring even to crawl out for a drink of water. It was the eleventh day before I ventured out from my hiding hole.

**CHAPTER 5**

# The Stillness

**ONCE** I made my way upstairs and slowly entered the kitchen, I found it empty. Every scrap of food was gone! The Martian had taken it all the previous day. I felt completely done in. I did not eat or even drink any water on the eleventh or the twelfth day.

At first, my mouth and throat were parched, and I felt myself getting weaker. My mind dwelled on eating. I thought I had become deaf—it seemed like the noises I had been hearing from the pit had stopped. I did not feel strong enough to crawl to the peephole.

On the twelfth day, my throat was so painful that I worked the creaking water pump that stood by the sink, and got a couple of glassfuls. I felt better after this, and felt a little safer, since no inquiring tentacle followed the noise of my pumping.

During these days, in a rambling, inconclusive way, I thought about the priest and of the manner of his death. On the thirteenth day, I drank some more water, slept and thought about eating and plans to escape. The light that came into the kitchen was no longer grey, but red. To my confused imagination, it seemed the color of blood.

On the fourteenth day, I went into the kitchen, and I was surprised to find that the red weed had grown right across the hole in the wall, turning the half-light of the place into a crimson-colored obscurity.

It was early on the fifteenth day that I heard curious, familiar sounds in the kitchen, and quickly identified them as the snuffing and scratching of a dog. Going into the kitchen, I saw a dog's nose peering in through a break in the wall. As he smelled me, he began to bark.

I thought if I could get him to come into the room, I might be able to kill him and have something to eat. In any case, I knew I had to silence him before his actions attracted the Martians.

I crept forward, saying "Good dog!" very softly; but he suddenly withdrew his head and disappeared. I listened but the pit was quiet. I heard the flutter of a bird's wings, but that was all.

For a long time, I lay close to the peephole, but not daring to move aside the red plants that obscured it. Once or twice, I heard the faint sounds of a dog wandering around on the sand below me, but that was all. After a while, encouraged by the silence, I looked out.

Except in one spot where a flock of crows fought over the bodies of the people the Martians had killed, there was not a living thing in the pit.

I stared around me, hardly believing my eyes. All the machinery was gone. Except for the big mound of blue powder over on one side, a few bars of metal scattered here and there, the black birds, and the skeletons of the dead, the place was an empty circular pit in the sand.

I crawled out of the hole and through the red weed plants and looked around. I could not see any sign of the Martians, so I knew my chance to escape had come. I scrambled to the top of the mound that covered the place where I had been buried and looked around.

The neighboring houses had all been wrecked, but none had been burned; their walls stood, sometimes to the second floor, with smashed windows and shattered doors. The red weed seemed to be growing everywhere up and down the street. It was in the front yards, in the back yards, and even grew in the demolished houses. Down in the pit, I saw where the crows were feasting on the bodies of the Martian's victims, but I saw no traces of living men.

The day seemed dazzlingly bright, the sky a glowing blue. A gentle breeze kept the red weed gently swaying. And oh! The sweetness of the open air!

**CHAPTER 6**

# The Work of Fifteen Days

I stood up on the mound looking over the landscape feeling free and alive. Inside that hiding place, I had thought of nothing except survival. I had not given a thought to what might be happening to the rest of the world, and I did not anticipate this startling unfamiliar landscape. I had expected to see the town in ruins but what I found all around me was the weird landscape of another planet as the hideous red plants seemed to be growing over everything.

I felt an anxiety far beyond the common emotions of men, but I imagine the poor brutes we dominate know it only too well. I felt like a rabbit might feel returning to his burrow and suddenly confronted by a dozen busy workmen digging the foundations for a new house. I felt a sense of dethronement, a concept that the human race was no longer master of Earth. We were now mere animals among all the other animals of the planet—all of us under the Martian heel. With us it would be like with the other animals, to lurk and watch, to run and hide—the empire of man had passed away.

But as soon as this strange thought went through my mind, it was gone, and my dominant concern became the hunger from my long and dismal fast. Away from the pit I saw a little patch of a green garden protected by stone walls. This gave me a goal, and I went knee-deep, and sometimes neck-deep, through the red weed. The density of the weed gave me a sense of hiding.

I finally found the garden, and stumbled into it so weak I was hardly able to climb over the top of its protecting wall. Once inside, I found some young onions, a couple of gladiolus bulbs, and a few carrots, all of which I gathered up and carried away. I passed through the mysterious Martian crimson vegetation with just two ideas: to get more food, and to get away from this unearthly region around the pit.

A little further on, I found a green grassy place, sat down, and devoured my meager harvest. Afterward, I came to a sheet of shallow weed-infested water where I previously had seen flat grasslands on the edge of the river. I discovered that it was caused by the unbelievably fast growth of the red weed. As soon as this alien plant got close to water, it immediately grew to gigantic proportions. Its seeds simply poured down into the water of any river or stream it found, and its quickly growing water fronds covered the entire expanse of the water. This effectively stopped the flow and caused the water to seek other paths and, of course, carried the red weed with it.

Later, I saw an entire bridge almost lost in a tangle of this weed. As the water spread, the weed followed it until the houses and other structures, and much of the destruction the Martians caused, were hidden in this red swamp.

In the end, the red weed died off almost as quickly as it had spread. A disease, due to bacteria, killed it off. All earthly plants have acquired resistance against these same bacterial diseases, but the red weed got sick and rotted like a thing already dead. The fronds became bleached almost white, and then quickly shriveled up and got brittle. They broke off at the lightest touch, and the waters that had stimulated their early growth carried their remains out to sea.

My first act on coming to this water was, of course, to satisfy my thirst. After that, I found the water shallow enough for me to wade, although the red weed interfered with my feet. After a while, I got out and made my way along a road going uphill.

As I walked along, the scenery changed from the strange red weed to the familiar wreckage where parts of neighborhoods looked like they had gone through a hurricane. A few yards later,

I would come to undisturbed spaces, houses with their blinds trimly drawn and doors closed, as if they had been left for a day by the owners, or as if their inhabitants slept inside. The red weed was less abundant, and the tall trees along the lane were free from the red creeper. I raided a couple of the silent houses, but they had already been ransacked. I rested for the remainder of the day, too fatigued to push on.

All this time, I saw no human beings, and no signs of the Martians. I encountered a couple of hungry-looking dogs, but they scurried away from me. Later, I saw two human skeletons—not bodies, but skeletons, picked clean.

After sunset, I struggled on along the road and eventually found a small garden. I dug up some potatoes, just enough to keep me going. From this garden, I looked down on a river. This part of the countryside seemed desolate: blackened trees, blackened, desolate ruins, and down the hill, the sheets of the flooded river, red-tinged with the weed. And over all—silence. It filled me with indescribable terror to think how swiftly this devastating change had come to my beloved country.

It seemed like mankind had been swept out of existence, and that I stood there alone, the last man left alive. As I walked on, I became more and more convinced that the extermination of mankind was, except for such stragglers as myself, already completed in this part of the world. I thought the Martians had destroyed the country and then gone on, seeking food somewhere else. Perhaps even now, they were destroying Berlin or Paris.

# CHAPTER 7

# The Man on the Hill

I spent that night in a small hotel, sleeping in a bed for the first time since my flight began. I will not tell you about the trouble I had breaking in, or how I ransacked every room for food. Just on the verge of despair, I found two tins of pineapple. Finally, in the bar, I found some biscuits and sandwiches that had been overlooked.

I was afraid to light a lamp, fearing some Martian might come looking around for food in the night. Before I went to bed, I felt restless, and prowled from window to window, searching for some sign of the monsters. I could not sleep. As I lay in bed, I found myself thinking. My brain, reinforced, I suppose, by the food I had eaten and relaxing, now that I was not in fear of my life, grew clear again, and I thought about what had happened to my world. Three things went through my mind: my actions with the priest, the whereabouts of the Martians, and the possible fate of my wife.

The priest and his capture caused me no feelings of horror or remorse. I saw it simply as a thing that had to be done. It was a very disagreeable act, but I did not have any choice. I saw myself then as I see myself now, driven step by step toward that hasty blow, the creature of a sequence of accidents leading inevitably to that act.

In the silence of the night, I stood my trial, my only trial, for that moment of wrath and fear. I retraced every one of our conversations from the moment when I first found him. I went over each of the situations we had experienced and my actions with him. My final thought is that the reader must judge me as he will.

After I got that picture of his prostrate body out of my mind, I faced the problem of the Martians and the fate of my wife. For the former, I had no information; I could imagine a hundred things, and so, unhappily, it was the same for the latter. And suddenly, the night and my loneliness became too terrible to bear. I found myself sitting up in bed, staring at the dark.

The morning's dawn was clear, and the eastern sky glowed pink, and was dotted with little golden clouds. On the road was a lot of evidence of the panicked flight that must have gone this way after the fighting began. There was a little cart with a smashed wheel and an abandoned trunk; there was a straw hat trampled into the now hardened mud; and at the top of the next hill, I saw a lot of blood-stained glass in front of a building. My movements through the area were slow, my plans unfocused.

I thought about looking for my wife, but I did not give myself much of a chance of finding her. Unless death had overtaken them suddenly, she and my cousin would have left his neighborhood, but where they might have gone, I could not guess. I knew I wanted to find my wife and that my heart ached for her, but I had no clear idea how it might be done. I now was sharply aware of my intense loneliness. I went, under cover of a thicket of trees and bushes, to the edge of a field, stretching away wide and far.

That dark expanse was dotted with patches of yellow flowers; there was no red weed to be seen. As I prowled on the edge of the open space, the sun rose, flooding it all with light and vitality. I came upon a bunch of little frogs in a swampy place among the trees. I stopped to look at them, drawing a lesson from their resolve to live. And then, with an odd feeling of being watched, I turned and saw something crouching amid a clump of bushes. I made a step toward it, and it rose up and became a man armed with a sword. I approached him slowly as he stood watching me, silent and motionless.

As I got closer, I saw he was dressed in clothes as dusty and filthy as my own; he looked like he had been dragged through a muddy ditch.

His black hair fell over his eyes, and his face was dark and dirty and sunken, so that at first I did not recognize him. There was a red cut across the lower part of his face.

"Stop!" he cried, when I was within ten yards of him. His voice was hoarse. "Where do you come from?" he demanded.

"I come from the south," I said. "I was buried near the pit the Martians made around their cylinder. I have worked my way out and escaped."

"There is no food around here," he said. "This is my country. All this hill down to the river, and back to the north up to the edge of that field. There is only food for one. Which way are you going?"

I answered slowly, "I don't know. I have been buried in the ruins of a house thirteen or fourteen days. I don't know what has happened."

He looked at me closely, turned to the side, and then jerked his head around and looked at me again with a changed expression.

"I've no wish to stop here," I said, stepping back a few feet. "I think I will go north. My wife was up there when this started."

He shot out a pointing finger and barked, "It is you! The man from the first cylinder! I thought you were killed at the bridge when I last saw you!"

I recognized him at the same moment and stammered, "You are the soldier who came into my garden!"

"Good grief!" he said. "Aren't we the lucky

ones! Fancy meeting YOU!" He put out a hand, and I took it. "I crawled up into a drain pipe," he said. "And they didn't kill everyone. After they left, I got away across the fields. But—it hasn't been sixteen days altogether—and your hair has turned gray!" He heard a noise and looked over his shoulder suddenly. "Only a bird," he said. "This is a bit in the open. Let us crawl under those bushes and talk."

"Have you seen any Martians?" I asked. "Since I crawled out . . ."

"They've gone across London to the north," he said. "I guess they've got a bigger camp there. All night, all over that area, the sky is alive with their lights. It's like a large city, and in the glare you can just barely see them moving. By daylight you can't. But I haven't seen them . . ." (he counted on his fingers) ". . . for five days. Then I saw two of them, across the way, carrying something big. And the night before last"—he stopped and spoke impressively—"I saw something up in the air. It was just lights, but I believe they've built a flying-machine, and are just now learning how to use it!"

I stopped, on hands and knees, as we were crawling under the bushes.

"Fly!"

"Yes," he said, "fly."

We went on into a little clearing under the bushes and sat down.

"It is all over for humanity," I said. "If they can fly, they will simply go around the world killing us all."

He nodded and added, "They will. But—if they fly away, it will relieve things for us around here for a while. And besides . . ." He looked at me. "Aren't you convinced it IS over for humanity? I am. We're down; we're beaten."

I stared. Strange as it may seem, I had not arrived at this fact—a fact perfectly obvious as soon as it came out of his mouth. I still held a vague hope. He repeated his words, "We're beaten." They carried absolute conviction.

"It's all over," he said. "They've lost ONE fighting machine—just ONE. And they've made their footing good and crippled England, the greatest power in the world. They've walked over us. The death of that one we saw was an accident. And these are only pioneers. They keep on coming. These green stars—I've not seen any the last five or six days, but I've no doubt they're falling somewhere every night. There is nothing to be done. We're down! We're beaten!"

I could not answer him. I sat staring at him, trying to think of some counter argument.

"This isn't a war," said the soldier. "It never was a war, any more than there's war between man and ants."

Suddenly, I recalled the night in the observatory so long ago when my friend and I watched

Mars through his telescope.

"After the tenth shot they did not fire any more—at least, until the first cylinder came."

"How do you know?" he asked, and I explained how I watched the planet Mars through a telescope.

He thought a moment and said, "Something went wrong with the gun. But so what if there is a problem? They'll fix it right soon enough. And even if there's a delay, how can it change the end result? It's just men and ants. The ants build their cities, live their lives, have wars, revolutions, until the men want them out of the way, and then they get moved out of the way. That's what we are now—just ants. Only . . ."

"Yes," I said.

"We're edible ants."

We sat looking at each other.

"So, what will they do with us?" I said.

"That's what I've been wondering," he said; "that's what I've been thinking about. After we got separated, I went south—thinking. I saw what was up. Most of the people were squealing and yelling. But I'm not so fond of squealing. I've been in sight of death once or twice. I'm not an ornamental soldier, and at the best and worst, death—it's just death. And it's the man that keeps on thinking—that's the one that comes through. I saw everyone running away from the south. I say, "Food won't last where they're going," and I turned right back around. All over the north"—he waved a hand toward the horizon—"men are starving in heaps, bolting, stomping on each other . . ."

He saw my face, apparently remembered my wife, and halted awkwardly.

"No doubt there're a lot of folks who had money that have escaped over to France," he said. He seemed about to apologize, met my eyes, and went on: "But there IS food all around here: canned things in shops, wines, spirits, mineral water in bottles. Well, I was telling you what I was thinking. They're intelligent things, but it seems they want us only for food. First, they'll smash us up—ships, machines, guns, cities, all the order and organization. All that will go. If we were the size of ants we might pull through. But we're not. Eh?"

I agreed.

"I've thought it out. Very well, then—next; at present we're caught just like they want. A Martian has only to go a few miles to get a crowd of people on the run. And I saw one, one day, picking houses to pieces and digging in the wreckage for something to eat. But they won't keep on doing that. As soon as they've destroyed all our guns and ships, and smashed our railways, and done all the things they are doing over there, they will begin catching us in a systematic way. They'll pick the best and store us in cages until they're ready. That's what they will start doing soon enough. Lord! They haven't even started on us yet. Don't you see that?"

"Not started!" I exclaimed.

"Not started. All that's happened so far is because we didn't have the sense to keep quiet—worrying them with guns and such stupidity. And losing our heads, and rushing off in crowds to where there wasn't any more safety than where we were in the first place. They don't want to bother us yet. They're making their machines—making all the things they couldn't bring with them, getting things ready for the rest of their people when they arrive. Very likely that's why the cylinders have stopped for a bit, for fear of hitting those who are here. And instead of our rushing around blind, or getting dynamite on the chance of blowing them up, we've got to fix ourselves up according to the new state of affairs. That's how I've figured it out. It isn't quite according to what a man wants for his species, but it's about what the facts point to. And that's the principle I acted upon. Cities, nations, civilization, progress—it's all over. That game's up. We're beat."

"But if that is so, what is there to live for?"

He looked at me for a moment and said, "There won't be any more blessed orchestra concerts for a million years or so, there won't be any Royal Academy of Arts, and no nice little dinners at restaurants. If it's amusement you're after, I reckon the game is up. If you've got any drawing room manners or a dislike of eating peas with a knife, you'd better throw them away. They ain't of no further use."

"You mean . . ."

"I mean that men like me will keep on living—for the sake of the breed. I tell you, I'm firm set on living as long as I can. And if I'm not mistaken, you'll show what kind of guts YOU'VE got, too, before long. We aren't going to be exterminated. And I don't mean to be caught either, and tamed and fattened and bred like a prize steer. Ugh!"

"You don't mean to say . . ."

"I do. I'm going on, under their feet. I've got it planned; I've thought it out. We men are beat. We don't know enough. We've got to learn a whole lot before we've got a chance. And we've got to live and keep independent while we learn. See! That's what has to be done."

I stared, astonished, and stirred profoundly by the man's resolution.

"Great God!" I cried. "You are a man indeed!" And suddenly I reached over and gripped his hand again.

"Eh!" he said, with his eyes shining. "I've thought it out, haven't I?"

"Go on," I said.

"Well, those who mean to escape the monsters must get ready. I'm getting ready. Mind

you, it isn't all of us who will be able to turn ourselves into wild beasts; but that's what we've got
to do. All these—the sort of people that lived in
these houses, and all those damn little clerks that
used to live down that way—they'd be no good.
They haven't any spirit in them—no proud
dreams and no proud lusts; and a man who hasn't
one or the other—Lord! What good is he?

"They just used to go off to work every
day—I've seen hundreds of 'em, bit of breakfast
in hand, running to catch their train, afraid
they'd get fired if they were late. They work at
businesses they were afraid to take the trouble to
understand. They hurry home for fear they won't
be in time for dinner and stay indoors after that
for fear of the streets. They sleep with the wives
they married, not because they want them, but
because the wife had a bit of money that would
make for safety in their one little miserable run
through the world. They've got life insurance
and a little savings account in case of an accident.

"And on Sundays—fear of the hereafter. As if
hell was built for rabbits! Well, the Martians will
just be a godsend to these folks. Nice roomy
cages, fattening food, careful breeding, no worry.
After a week or so, chasing around the fields and
woods on empty stomachs, they'll come and be
caught with no problem."

He paused.

"Very likely these Martians will make pets of

some of them; train them to do tricks—who knows? Maybe some . . . they will train to hunt us."

"No," I cried, "that's impossible! No human being . . ."

"What's the good of going on with such lies?" snapped the soldier. "There's men who'd do it with a smile on their face. What nonsense to pretend there isn't!"

And I gave in to his conviction.

I sat thinking about these things. I could find nothing to argue against this man's reasoning. In the days before the invasion, no one would have questioned my intellectual superiority to his. I mean, I am a university professor and recognized writer on philosophical themes, and he is but a common soldier, and yet he had already figured out a situation that I had barely realized.

"What are you doing about it?" I said after a pause. "What plans have you made?"

He hesitated.

"Well, it's like this," he said. "What do we have to do? We have to invent a sort of life where men can live and breed, and be secure enough to raise children. Yes—wait a bit, and I'll make it more clear what I think ought to be done. The tame ones will go like all tame beasts—to the slaughter. In a few generations, they'll be big, beautiful, rich-blooded, stupid—cattle!

"The risk is that we who escape the monsters

will go savage—degenerate into a sort of big, ferocious rat . . . You see, how I mean to live is underground. I've been thinking about the sewers. Of course, those who don't know drains think horrible things; but under London are miles and miles—hundreds of miles—of pipes and culverts. After just a few days of rain, with London being empty of people, the whole sewer system will be sweet and clean. The main drains are big enough and airy enough for anyone. Then there's cellars, vaults, stores, from which connecting passages may be made to the drains. And, of course, there are also the railway and subways tunnels. Eh? You begin to see? And we form a band—able-bodied, clean-minded men. We're not going to keep any weaklings that just drift in. Troublemakers will get thrown out.

"Those who stay will obey orders. Able-bodied, clean-minded women we want also—mothers and teachers. No fancy, painted ladies who are lazy or good for nothing—we don't need their pouting faces and rolling eyes. We can't have any weak or silly females. Life is real again, and the useless and cumbersome and mischievous have to die. They ought to die. They ought to be willing to die. It's a sort of disloyalty, after all, to live and taint the race. And they would never be happy. Good grief, dying is not so dreadful.

"Our district will be London. And we may even be able to keep a watch, and run around in the open when the Martians aren't around. Play cricket, perhaps. That's how we shall save the race. Eh? It's a possible thing?

"But saving the race is nothing in itself. As I say, that's only being rats. It's saving our knowledge and adding to it—that is the thing. That is where men like you come in. There are books we must protect. We must make safe places down deep, and get all the books we can; not novels and poetry trash, but ideas, science books. That's where men like you come in.

"We must go to the British Museum and college libraries and pick out all those books we might need. Especially, we must keep up our science—and learn more. We must watch these Martians and learn from them. Some of us must go to them as spies. When we are all working and set up, perhaps I'll give that a try. Get caught, I mean. And the great thing is, we must leave the Martians alone. We should not even steal from them. If we get in their way, we clear out. We must show them we mean no harm. Yes, I know. But they're intelligent things, and they won't hunt us down if they have all they want and think we're just harmless vermin."

He paused, reached out and grabbed my arm as he said, "After all, we may not need to learn too much before we start to fight 'em back! Just imagine this: four or five of their fighting machines suddenly starting off—Heat Rays blastin' right and left, and not a Martian in 'em. Not a Martian in 'em, but men—men who have learned how to operate 'em! It may be in our time, it may be the next generation. Imagine having one of those lovely things, with its Heat Ray, running around wide and free! Imagine having it under your control! What would it matter if you smashed it to smithereens at the end of the run, after a rampage like that? I reckon that would open the Martians' eyes! Can't you see them, man? Can't you see them hurrying, hurrying—puffing and blowing and hooting to their other mechanical contraptions? And swish, bang, rattle, swish! Just as they are fumbling around, SWISH comes the Heat Ray, and, behold! Man has come back to his own!"

For a while, the daring of the soldier, and his tone of assurance and courage, completely dominated my mind. I believed in both his faith in human destiny and in the feasibility of his astonishing scheme. We talked through the morning, and later crept out of the bushes. After scanning for Martians, we hurried to the house where he had made his lair.

We went down into the basement, and I saw the work he had been doing—it was a tunnel about ten yards long. When he said it would soon reach the main drain under the street, I had my first inkling of the gulf between his dreams and his powers. I knew I could dig a hole like this in one day. But I believed in him enough to work with him all that morning. For lunch we had ourselves a can of soup and some wine from the pantry. I found relief from the aching strangeness of the outside world in this steady labor. As we worked, I turned his project over in my mind and came up with some objections and doubts; but I worked there all morning anyway, happy to find myself with a purpose again.

After a while I began to speculate on the distance we had to go before we reached the main drain, and wondered about the chances of missing it altogether. My immediate problem was why we had to dig this long tunnel, when it was possible to get into the main drain down one of the manholes out in the street. In addition, it seemed to me that this house was inconveniently chosen, and required a longer length of tunnel than another house just down the street. And just as I was beginning to face these things, the soldier stopped digging, and looked at me.

"We've done well," he said as he put down his spade. "Let's take a break. I think it's time we took a look from the roof of the house."

"But the work?"

"Oh, one can't always work," he said, and in a flash I saw through the man plain as day—no wonder the tunnel wasn't completed. He hesitated and said, "We ought to go and take a look now, because if anyone comes near they may hear the shovels and sneak up on us."

We went up to the flat roof and gazed out. No Martians were to be seen, and we ventured out and hid behind a parapet.

From this position, we could see the river below, a bubbly mass of red weed, and the low parts of the town flooded and red. The red creeper swarmed up the trees around a fancy house, and their branches stretched gaunt and dead, with shriveled leaves grouped in clusters. It was strange how entirely dependent both the weed and the creeper were upon flowing water for their propagation. Around us, in this neighborhood with its higher elevation, neither Martian plant had gained a footing; our native plants surrounded us in abundance in the sunlight. A few miles away we saw dense smoke and a blue haze that hid the northern hills.

The soldier began to tell me about the people who still remained in London, "One night last week, some fools got the electric power working again, and all along the main street it was lit up, crowded with painted and ragged drunkards, men and women, dancing and shouting till dawn. A man who was there told me. And as the morning came they saw a fighting machine standing near by and looking down at them. Heaven knows how long he had been there. It must have given some of them a nasty turn. The Martian came over toward them and picked up nearly a hundred fools too drunk or frightened to run away."

After a pause, he started talking about his grand plans again. He grew enthusiastic. He talked so eloquently of the possibility of capturing a fighting machine that I more than half believed in him again. But now that I was beginning to understand him better, I could see he was not going to do anything too quickly. And I noted that now there was no question that it was he, personally, who planned to capture the great fighting machine and turn it on the Martians.

After a time, we went down to the cellar. Neither of us seemed to want to resume digging, and when he suggested a meal, I was more than ready. He suddenly became very generous, and when we had finished eating, he went away and returned with some excellent cigars. We lit these, and his optimism glowed along with the cigar tips. He was inclined to regard my coming as a great occasion.

"There's some champagne hidden over there," he said, pointing to a corner.

"We can dig better on this burgundy," was my reply.

"No, I am host today. Champagne! Great God! We've got enough work ahead of us! Let's take a rest and gather strength while we can. Look at these blistered hands!"

And continuing this idea of a lunchtime

break, he insisted on playing cards after we had eaten. Grotesque and foolish as this will seem to the sober reader, it is absolutely true, and what is more remarkable, I found the card game we played extremely interesting.

Strange is the mind of man! With our species on the edge of extermination, with no clear prospect in front of us but the chance of a horrible death, we could sit and play cards with delight. When dark came, we decided to take the risk and lit a lamp.

After an interminable string of games, we ate again and finished the champagne. We went on smoking the cigars. He was no longer the energetic regenerator of his species I had encountered in the morning. He was still optimistic, but it was a less active, a more thoughtful optimism. I took a cigar, and went upstairs to look at the lights that blazed so brightly along the hills.

I stared across the London valley. The northern hills were shrouded in darkness; the fires to the east glowed, and now and then an orange-red tongue of flame flashed up and vanished in the deep blue night. All the rest of London was black. Then, nearer, I saw a strange light, a pale, violet-purple fluorescent glow, quivering in the night breeze. For a moment, I could not understand it, and then I knew that it must be coming from the red weed. With that realization, my dormant sense of wonder, my sense of the way of the world, awoke again. I glanced from that up to the heavens to see Mars, red and clear, glowing high in the west, and then gazed back down at the darkness of the city in the distance.

I stayed up on the roof for a long time, thinking about the day. I recalled my mental states from my midnight thoughts to the foolish cardplaying a short while ago. I suddenly felt revulsion at what I had been doing all day. My thoughtlessness hit me like a blow. I felt like I was a traitor to my wife and to my kind; I was filled with remorse. I decided to leave this strange undisciplined dreamer of great things to his drink and gluttony, and to go on into London. There, it seemed to me, I had the best chance of learning what the Martians and my fellowmen were doing. I was still on the roof when the moon rose.

**CHAPTER 8**

# Dead London

I left the soldier's house and made my way toward London. The red weed was still growing at that time and nearly choked the roadway on either side of a small bridge. But I noticed that its fronds were already whitened in patches by the spreading disease that soon would kill it off.

There was black dust along the roadway from the bridge onward, and it grew thicker as I went along. The streets were horribly quiet. I got food—sour, hard, and moldy, but edible—in a baker's shop. After a while, the streets became clear of the black dust, and I passed a group of houses on fire; the noise of the burning was an absolute relief. A few blocks past them, the streets were quiet again.

I went into another area and saw black dust in the streets again and this time saw a few dead bodies. They had been dead many days, and I went past them quickly. The black dust covered them completely and softened their outlines. It looked like dogs had disturbed one or two of them.

Where there was no black dust, it was like a Sunday in the city, with the closed shops, the houses locked up and the blinds drawn, the desertion, and the stillness. Some places had been plundered, but it seemed only the food stores and wine shops had been hit. A jeweler's window had been broken open in one place, but apparently the thief had been disturbed, and a number of gold chains and a watch lay scattered on the pavement. Farther on I saw a tattered woman on a doorstep; the hand that hung over her knee was gashed and bled down her rusty brown dress, and a smashed magnum of champagne formed a pool across the pavement. She seemed asleep, but she was dead.

The stillness grew more oppressive the farther I went into London. But it was not so much the stillness of death—it was the stillness of suspense, of expectation. At any time, the destruction that had singed the northwestern borders of the metropolis and had annihilated the southern suburbs, might strike among these houses and leave them smoking ruins. It was a city condemned and abandoned.

As I went along further, the streets were clear of both dead people and the black dust. I wondered if I was imagining things when I first heard the howling. It crept almost imperceptibly into my senses. It was a sobbing alternation of two notes, "Ulla, ulla, ulla, ulla," repeating itself over and over again with no change. When I passed streets that ran northward, it got louder. It came full blast down one broad avenue. I stopped, staring to the north, wondering about this strange, remote wailing. It was as if that mighty desert of houses had found a voice for its fear and solitude.

"Ulla, ulla, ulla, ulla," wailed that superhuman note—great waves of sound sweeping down the broad, sunlit roadway, with its tall buildings on each side. I turned north toward the sound. All the large mansions on each side of the road were empty and still, and my footsteps echoed against the sides of the houses before I entered a well-maintained park. The voice grew stronger and stronger, though I could see nothing above the housetops on the north side of the park except for a haze of smoke.

"Ulla, ulla, ulla, ulla," cried the voice, coming, as it seemed to me, from just a few blocks away. The desolating cry was doing weird things to my mind. The mood that had sustained me passed away. The wailing voice took possession of me. I found I was weary, footsore, and now hungry and thirsty again.

It was already past noon. Why was I wandering alone in this city of the dead? Why was I here when all of London was lying in state in its black shroud? I felt intolerably lonely. My mind wandered to old friends that I had not seen for years. I wondered if anyone else shared the city with me  . . .

I came into another small park I remembered from prior times, and found more black dust and several bodies, and an evil, ominous smell coming from the broken windows of some of the houses. I managed to break into a diner and get some food and drink. I was weary after eating and slept in one of the booths.

I awoke to find that dismal howling still in my ears, "Ulla, ulla, ulla, ulla." It was now dusk, and after I packed away some biscuits and cheese, I wandered north toward the strange sound. Finally, I saw the Martian fighting machine that was making the noise. I was not terrified. I came up on him as if it were a matter of course. I watched him for some time, but he did not move. He appeared to be standing and yelling for no reason.

I tried to formulate a plan of action. That perpetual sound of "Ulla, ulla, ulla, ulla," confused my mind. Perhaps I was too tired to be frightened. Certainly I was more curious to know the reason for this monotonous noise than I was afraid. I went along under the shelter of some terraces, and got a closer view of this stationary, howling Martian. A couple of hundred yards away I heard a yelping chorus, and saw a dog with a piece of red meat in his jaws coming headlong toward me, followed by a pack of starving mongrels in pursuit of him. He made a wide curve to avoid me, as though he feared I might prove a fresh competitor. As the yelping of the dogs died away down the silent road, the wailing sound of "Ulla, ulla, ulla, ulla," reasserted itself.

I came upon a wrecked spider-machine. At first I thought a house had fallen across the road. It was only as I climbed over the ruins that I saw the mechanical monster, with its tentacles bent and smashed and twisted, lying among the ruins it had made. The front was shattered. It seemed like it had driven straight into the house and had been crushed as the house collapsed on top of it. It looked to me like the Martian operator had lost control of the machine.

Wondering about these stationary machines, I pushed on. Far away, through a gap in the trees, I saw a second Martian fighting machine, as motionless as the first, standing, silently, in a park. As I walked toward it, the sound of "Ulla, ulla, ulla, ulla," stopped. The silence came like a thunderclap.

The houses around me stood tall and dim; the trees toward the park were growing black. Night, the mother of fear and mystery, was coming. But while that voice sounded, the solitude and desolation had been endurable. Because of that noise, London had still seemed alive, and the sense of life around me had kept me going. Then suddenly a change, the passing of something—I did not know what—and then a stillness that could be felt. There was nothing but this extreme quiet.

All London seemed to gaze at me. The windows in the houses were like the eye sockets of skulls. My imagination found a thousand noiseless enemies moving in the shadows. Terror seized me. In front, the road became pitch black, and I saw a contorted shape lying up on the left. I could not bring myself to go on past the dead body. I turned away and ran from this unendurable stillness. I hid from the night and the silence in a church whose doors were wide open. But before the dawn my courage returned, and while the stars were still in the sky, I turned back to where I had walked last night. As I crested a hill, I saw a third Martian, towering up to the fading stars, standing tall and motionless like the others.

An insane resolve possessed me. I would die and end it. And I would save myself even the trouble of killing myself. I marched recklessly toward this Titan, and then, as I drew nearer and the light got brighter, I saw that a flock of black birds was circling and clustering around the hood. At that sight my heart gave a bound, and I began running along the road toward the park ahead.

I ran out onto the grass with the rising sun blazing in front of me. High dirt mounds had been heaped around the crest of the hill, making a huge protective wall—it was the largest Martian encampment that I had seen. Behind the heaps, I could see a thin stream of smoke rising up against the sky. The thought that had flashed into my mind began to grow real, and slowly grew conceivable. I felt no fear, only a wild, trembling exultation as I ran up the hill toward the motionless monster. Lank brown meat seemed to be hanging out of the hood, and that was what the hungry birds were pecking and tearing at.

I scrambled up the earth rampart and stood on its crest. I saw the interior of the pit spread out below me. It was a large space containing gigantic machines here and there, huge mounds of material and strange shelter-like places. Scattered around, some in their overturned war-machines, some in the now stationary spider-machines, and a dozen of them laid out in a row, were the Martians—DEAD! They were killed by the bacteria against which their systems were unprepared; slain just like the red weed was being slain; slain, after all man's devices had failed, by the humblest things that God, in his wisdom, has put on this earth.

For so it had come about, as indeed I and many others might have foreseen if terror and disaster had not blinded our minds. These disease germs have taken toll of humanity since the beginning of time—taken toll of our pre-human ancestors since life began here. But by virtue of the natural selection of our kind, we have developed resistance to these diseases. We do not succumb to our common germs without a struggle, and to many—those that cause decay in dead matter, for instance—our living bodies are completely immune.

But there are no bacteria on Mars, and as soon as these invaders arrived, as soon as they drank and fed and breathed our air, our microscopic allies began to work on their overthrow. Even when I first watched them, they were doomed, dying and rotting as they went to and fro. It was inevitable. By paying the toll of a billion deaths, man has bought his birthright from these organisms of the earth, and it is his against all comers; it would still be his even if the Martians were ten times as mighty.

The dead Martians were scattered all over the pit, nearly fifty of them altogether. They were overtaken by a death that must have seemed incomprehensible to them. All I knew was that these things that had been alive and so terrible to men were now dead.

I stood staring into the pit, and my heart lightened gloriously, even as the rising sun lit up the world around me with its rays. The pit was still in darkness; the mighty machines, so great and wonderful in their power and complexity, so unearthly in their form, rose weird and vague and strange out of the shadows toward the light. I could hear a mass of dogs fighting over the bodies that lay in the depths of the pit, far below me. Across the pit on its farther lip, flat and vast and strange, lay the immense flying-machine that they had been working on. Death had come not a day too soon. At the sound of crows cawing overhead, I looked up at the huge fighting machine that would fight no more and at the tattered shreds of flesh that dripped down to the ground.

I turned and looked over at the masses of birds crowded around the other two Martian fighting machines that I had seen overnight, just as death had overtaken them. The one had died as it had been calling to its companions; perhaps it was the last to die, and its voice had gone on until the energy of its machinery was exhausted. They glittered now, harmless tripod towers of shining metal, in the brightness of the rising sun, as the birds feasted.

All around the pit, and saved from everlasting destruction, stretched the great Mother of Cities, London. Those who have only seen London veiled in her dark robes of smoke can not imagine the naked clearness and beauty of the silent wilderness of houses that I saw that day.

To the east, over some blackened ruins and the splintered spire of a church, the sun blazed in a clear sky, and here and there some facet in the great wilderness of roofs caught the light and glared with a white intensity.

And as I looked around, north, south, east, and west, at this wide expanse of houses and factories and churches, now silent and abandoned, I thought of the multitude of hopes and efforts, the innumerable lives that had gone to build this great city, and of the swift and ruthless destruction that had hung over it all. I realized that the shadow had been rolled back, and that men could again live in these streets, and this dear, vast, dead city of mine could once more be alive and powerful. I felt a wave of emotion that was close to tears.

The torment was over. Even that day, the healing would begin. The survivors of the people scattered over the country—leaderless, lawless, foodless, like sheep without a shepherd—the thousands who had fled by sea, would begin to return. The pulse of life, growing stronger and stronger, would beat again in the empty streets and pour across the vacant squares and parks. Whatever destruction was done, the hand of the destroyer was stopped.

All the wreckage, the blackened skeletons of houses that stared so dismally at the sunlit grass of the hill, would soon be echoing with the hammers of the restorers and ringing with the tapping of their trowels. At the thought, I extended my hands toward the sky and began thanking God. All this could be repaired in a year, I thought—in a year. . . .

Then, with overwhelming force, came the thought of myself, of my wife, and the old life of hope and tender helpfulness that had NOT ceased forever. We had been given another chance.

# CHAPTER 9

# Wreckage

**AND** now comes the strangest part of my story.
Yet, perhaps, it is not entirely strange. I remember, clearly and vividly, everything that I did that
day until after I stood up on the top of that hill
weeping and thanking God. And, after that, I for-
get.

Of the next three days, I remember nothing.
I have since learned that, far from my being the
first to discover the downfall of the Martians, several such wanderers as myself had already seen
this on the previous night. One man had gone to
a telegraph office and managed to send word to
Paris. After that, the joyful news had flashed all
over the world; a thousand cities had been told
the good news by the time I stood at the edge of
the pit.

Men were already setting up trains to take
people back to London, though some were
weeping with joy as they worked. The church
bells that had been stopped for two weeks were

suddenly starting up again, until all England was bell-ringing. Men went along every country lane shouting about the deliverance, shouting to gaunt, staring figures of despair.

And the food! Across the Channel, across the Irish Sea, across the Atlantic, corn, bread, and meat were coming to our relief. All the shipping in the world seemed to be going toward London in those days. But of all this, I have no memory. I drifted—a demented man. I found myself in a house of kindly people, who had found me on the third day, wandering, weeping, and raving through the streets. They told me that I was singing, "The Last Man Left Alive! Hurrah! The Last Man Left Alive!" Troubled as they were with their own affairs, these people sheltered me and protected me from myself.

Very gently, when my mind was back to sanity again, they broke the news to me of what they had learned about Smithville. They told me it had been destroyed, along with every soul in it. A Martian had swept it out of existence without any provocation, like a boy might crush an anthill.

I was a lonely man, and they were very kind to me. I stayed with them for a few days after my recovery. All that time I felt a vague, growing desire to look once more on whatever remained of my life back in my hometown. They did all they could to divert me from this morbid quest.

But at last I could not resist, and parting from these recent friends with tears, I went out again into the streets that had lately been so dark and strange and empty. Already they were busy with returning people; in places there were shops open, and I even saw a drinking fountain with running water.

I remember how bright the day seemed as I went on my sad pilgrimage back to my little house. So many people were out everywhere, busy at a thousand activities, that it seemed incredible that a large percentage of the population could have been killed. The churches were distributing bread sent us by the French government. The ribs of horses showed dismally. Haggard policemen stood at the corners of every street. I saw little of the damage caused by the Martians until I reached the southern suburbs, and there I saw extensive wreckage and the remains of the red weed.

At a railway station, I found the trains that were taking people to their homes. The first rush was already over. There were few people in the train, and I was in no mood for casual conversation. I sat with folded arms, looking at the sunlit devastation that flowed past the windows. Parts of southern London were still coated with the black smoke's dust, in spite of two days of thunderstorms and rain.

I got off the train at my stop and walked

through the familiar woods, neck-high with red weed here and there. I came to my house with a quick flash of hope that faded immediately. The door had been forced open, and it was swinging with the wind as I approached.

The curtains of my study fluttered out of the open window. The smashed bushes were just as I had left them so long ago. I stumbled into the hall, and the house felt empty. The stair carpet was ruffled and discolored where I had crouched, soaked to the skin from the thunderstorm the first night of the catastrophe. The evidence of muddy footsteps went up the stairs.

I followed them to my study, and found my writing table with the papers I had left there that horrible afternoon so long ago. I remembered my inability to concentrate that morning, scarcely a month gone by, and how I had stopped and gone off to get my newspaper. I remembered how I went down to the garden gate as the newsboy came along, and how I had listened to his odd story of "Men from Mars."

I walked downstairs and went into the dining room. My home was desolate. I realized the foolishness of the faint hope I had cherished for so long. And then a strange thing occurred. "It is no use," said a man's voice outside. "The house is deserted. No one has been here for days. Do not stay here to torment yourself. No one escaped but you."

I was startled. Had I spoken my thought out loud? I turned, and the French doors were open onto the patio. I stepped over and looked out.

And there, amazed and afraid, even as I stood amazed and afraid, were my cousin and my wife—my wife! She gave a faint cry.

"I came," she said. "I knew—knew—"

She put her hand to her throat—swayed. I dashed forward and caught her in my arms.

**CHAPTER 10**

# The Epilogue

**THE** bacteria theory as the cause of the rapid death of the Martians seems most probable to me. I regret how little I was able to take part in the many discussions related to the Martian invasion and its aftermath.

At any rate, in all the bodies of the Martians that were examined after the war, only our good old terrestrial bacteria species were found.

The composition of the black smoke, which the Martians used with such deadly effect, remains a puzzle. Spectrum analysis of the black dust indicates the presence of an unknown element. Scientists and engineers have made no progress in deciphering the complexities of the Heat Ray generator or any of the other Martian machines and weapons.

I have already described the results of an anatomical examination of the Martians. But everyone is familiar with the magnificent and almost complete specimen displayed at the

Natural History Museum.

A question of graver and universal interest is the possibility of another attack by the Martians. I do not think that enough attention is being given to this aspect of the matter. In any case, we should be prepared. It seems to me that it should be possible to keep a sustained watch on Mars and to anticipate the arrival of the next attack.

In that case, the cylinders might be destroyed before they were cool enough for the Martians to emerge, or they might be killed as soon as the cylinders opened. It seems to me that they have lost a tremendous advantage in the failure of their first surprise attack. Possibly they see it in the same light.

Anyway, whether we expect another invasion or not, our views of the human future must be reevaluated in light of these events. We have learned now that we cannot think of our planet as being fenced in and a secure place for Man. We can never anticipate the unseen good or evil that may come to us from space.

It may be that in the larger design of the universe, this invasion from Mars is not without its ultimate benefit for men. Though it may have robbed us of some of our confidence in the future, the gifts to human science it has brought are enormous, and it has done much to promote the concept of the common plight of mankind.

The broadening of men's views can scarcely

be exaggerated. Before the cylinders fell, there was a consensus that throughout outer space no life existed except on the surface of our planet. Now we know better. If the Martians can reach our planet, then perhaps men can reach other planets, as well. When the slow cooling of the sun eventually makes our Earth uninhabitable, it may be that the thread of life that has begun here will have streamed out and caught other planets in its coils.

I have a wonderful vision of life spreading slowly from our little part of the solar system throughout the vastness of space. But that is a remote dream. It may be, on the other hand, that the destruction of the Martians is only a reprieve. Perhaps the future is promised to them, and not to us.

I must confess the stress and danger of the time have left a profound sense of doubt in my mind. I sit in my study writing by lamplight, and suddenly I see the beautiful valley below again covered in flames, and feel the houses around me empty and desolate. I go to London and see the busy crowds in the streets, and it flashes through my mind that they are the ghosts of the past, haunting the streets that I have seen silent, empty, and wretched.

And strangest of all is to hold my wife's hand again, and to remember that I had counted her, and that she had counted me, among the dead.

AFTERWORD

# About the Author

**IF** you were asked to explain "science fiction" to someone who had never before heard the term, what would you say?

The chances are good that you would mention such familiar elements as time travel, alien invasions, killer robots, flying saucers, death rays, and interplanetary war.

Whether you knew it or not, such a description would owe its existence to H.G. (Herbert George) Wells, the man who almost single-handedly invented modern science fiction. His novels, including such classics as *The War of the Worlds*, *The Time Machine*, and *The Invisible Man*, introduced science fiction concepts that are now so familiar it is impossible to imagine the genre without them.

How did a person like Wells, an Englishman born of lower-class parents during the reign of Queen Victoria, not only dream up brilliantly imaginative concepts, but imagine unheard-of things *that would soon become reality*? For while Wells was considered a fantasy writer in his time, he is seen today as a prophet as well. There seems no good answer to the question. History teaches us that occasionally a person like Wells comes along—a person so advanced in his thinking, so seemingly untethered by the restrictions of the era he lives in that there is simply no explanation for him.

Wells was born in 1866 in Bromley, a village outside of London. He was the youngest of five children. His father, Joseph, worked as a gardener and later as a shopkeeper. Primarily, though, he supported himself playing cricket, a popular British sport that vaguely resembles baseball. His mother, Sarah, worked as a lady's maid. The family struggled to pay the bills.

Little about young Herbert's upbringing suggested that he would become a world-famous author and thinker. Looking back, only two facts stand out. One is that when Herbert was seven, he suffered a broken leg and had to stay in bed for some time. With little else to do, the young boy discovered a love of reading, and began to dream about writing his own stories someday. Secondly, his mother was employed at a rich man's country house that included a magnificent library. Occasionally Herbert was allowed to stay at the house while his mother worked. There he spent his time enjoying the great collection of books.

When Herbert was only eleven, another accident affected his life. His father fractured his thigh, putting an end to his career as a cricket-player. With that income gone, the wolf was truly at the Wells's door. Like his older brothers, Herbert was soon taken out of school and sent out to work as an apprentice to various "masters." The first was a man who ran a clothing store; Herbert hated the business. The next was a pharmacist. Herbert also did poorly in that line of work.

Fortunately for Herbert, who had continued to read voraciously, he lived in an era when self-educated people were judged more on their abilities than by their academic degrees. He was able to land a position as an assistant teacher at a local grammar school. From there he won a scholarship to study zoology at the Royal College of Science. In college, Wells began to find his natural environment, and his love of reading and study asserted itself. He was deeply influenced by his teachers, particularly his biology professor, T.H. Huxley. Huxley was a well-known scientist and a champion of Charles Darwin's theories of evolution. (An interesting note is that T.H. Huxley's grandson, Aldous Huxley, wrote the famous novel *Brave New World*. Like much of Wells's writing, that novel deals with the imagined future of humanity.)

In 1891 at the age of twenty-five, Wells married a cousin, Isabel. He then devoted his attention to writing full time, with his first work being a textbook on biology. As it turned out, marriage and family life were not Wells's strong point. Three years after his marriage to Isabel, he ran off with a former student, Amy Catherine Robbins. He and Amy married and remained married until Amy's death, although Wells had highly public affairs with many other women. He fathered children with two of them; one was a well-known novelist and feminist, Rebecca West, who was 26 years his junior.

In 1895, Wells burst on the public scene as a notable author with the publication of *The Time Machine*. In this novel, Wells popularized the notion that time travel could occur in a machine that traveled beyond the known three-dimensional universe. This was more than 50 years before Einstein wrote of the concept of time as the fourth dimension. The very next year, Wells again astounded the reading public with his novel *The Island of Dr. Moreau*. In it he imagines a mad scientist who has created a strange race of man-creatures, surgically altering animals to make them more human-like. With any idea of genetic engineering a hundred years in the future, the concept was both novel and terrifying. Wells followed this triumph in 1897 with *The Invisible Man*. This is another scary story of science run amok, as a scientist who has discovered the secret of invisibility descends into insanity.

And in 1898, on the heels of the announcement that "canals" had been discovered on Mars (actually the word was a mistranslation of the Italian for "channels," which more accurately described what astronomers could see), Wells published his most famous novel: *The War of the Worlds*. Because of the mistranslation, rumors were widespread that intelligent Martians had created artificial canals on the planet's surface. As a result, readers were more than ready to accept the idea of an invasion by men from Mars.

Wells wrote two more science fiction novels—*The First Men on the Moon*, which quite accurately imagined space flight, and *The War in the Air*, which foresaw the use of air forces in combat. He then turned to more realistic novels, which also found a wide audience.

Perhaps Wells's most remarkable feat of prophesying occurred when he wrote his 1914 novel, *The World Set Free*. It is not one of his best-known books, but it is amazing in the accuracy with which it foresees the development of the atomic bomb. In it he writes:

> Certainly it seems now that nothing could have been more obvious to the people of the earlier twentieth century than the rapidity with which war was becoming impossible. And as certainly they did not see it. They did not see it until the atomic bombs burst in their fumbling hands. . . .

Poignantly, Wells lived to see his words come true. On August 6, 1945, 41 years after he wrote the above passage, a U.S. Air Force bomber dropped the atomic bomb on Hiroshima. The bombing killed an estimated 200,000 people and brought about the surrender of Japan in World War II. One year later, on August 13, 1946, the writer and prophet H.G. Wells died peacefully in London.

## About the Book

IT'S impossible to talk about *The War of the Worlds* without mentioning what happened the evening of October 30, 1938. H.G. Wells's novel was already forty years old and famous in its own right. But what occurred that Halloween week would move *The War of the Worlds* from the realm of "famous" into "notorious."

In 1938, radio was the most powerful medium on earth. Millions of people listened to popular radio shows every day. Entire families gathered around the radio, much as they would around television sets a few decades later. Dramas, comedies, soap operas, and variety shows were all popular offerings. Perhaps because fans could only hear what was happening, and had to provide pictures in their imaginations,

they became tremendously involved in the pro-
grams, at least as much as TV watchers do today.

This was the atmosphere on that autumn
Sunday night when listeners tuned in to CBS
Radio. They were enjoying a program of dance
music, live from the Park Plaza in New York City,
when an announcer broke in with startling news.
Enormous blue flames, he said, had been spotted
shooting up from the surface of Mars.

The dance program continued, but the
announcer broke in again: A meteor had fallen to
Earth in Grovers Mill, New Jersey. No, wait, he
reported with rising excitement—it wasn't a
meteor at all. It was a cylinder of some kind, and
from it emerged a terrifying creature which
destroyed onlookers with some sort of heat ray!

With that announcement, the most famous
night in radio history got underway. Countless
listeners gathered around their radios, listening
with rising terror to the "breaking news story"
about a Martian invasion of Earth.

Panic swept over the New York-New Jersey
area, where the Martians had supposedly landed.
According to the next day's *New York Times*,
more than twenty families in one Newark neighborhood rushed into the street, their faces covered with wet towels, trying to escape what they
thought would be a gas raid. Thousands of people placed hysterical calls to the police, asking for
guidance. Dozens more were admitted to hospi-

tals, suffering from symptoms of shock. Churches filled with worshippers, weeping and praying, believing the world was about to end.

Of course, it was all just a radio play—a dramatization of Wells's novel, set in the United States instead of England. At the beginning of the broadcast, and at three times during the course of it, the announcement was made that listeners were hearing a performance by actor Orson Welles and his Mercury Theatre. Of course, most listeners realized what they were hearing and merely enjoyed the astonishing realism of the show. But thousands others were all but maddened with panic.

As the news spread the following day that the "invasion" had been merely a radio show, many people were infuriated at what they thought had been an irresponsible stunt. Public outrage was so great that within weeks, the Federal Communication Commission had forbidden radio shows from using the "open format"—that is, pretending to break into ordinary programming.

From the vantage point of the early twenty-first century, the terror inspired by *The War of the Worlds* broadcast seems extreme, even silly. But there are at least two reasons why the listeners' panic is understandable.

The first and simplest reason is that many listeners tuned in late to the broadcast, missing the first announcement that what they were about to hear was merely a play. By the time the subsequent announcements were made, those people who were prone to panic were probably in no state to comprehend them.

But more importantly, in October 1938, the world was a tension-filled place. The Great Depression that had begun in 1929 and continued through most of the 1930s was still very much on people's minds. They were shaken by the way the stable world they had once known had crumbled. In Europe, dictators Adolf Hitler and Benito Mussolini were gathering strength in Germany and Italy. War was in the air; in fact Nazi Germany would invade Poland, thus setting off World War II, in just eleven months. After the panic of the broadcast died down, many listeners said they had assumed the "Martian" invasion was actually a cleverly disguised German attack.

Although H.G. Wells was not pleased that his novel had been the source of a panic in America, he must have taken some ironic satisfaction in what happened. For one of the strongest influences on Wells as he wrote *The War of the Worlds* was his passionate belief in Charles Darwin's theory of evolution.

Darwin's work was still relatively new and very controversial when Wells wrote his novel. The two men's shared belief that all species evolved through the process of natural selection, with the strong eventually overcoming the weak, flew in the face of the more widespread belief in a kindly, just world overseen by an all-knowing God.

Evidence of Wells's passionate belief in evolution is seen throughout *The War of the Worlds*. In the earliest pages of the novel, he makes it clear that he does not regard the Martians as the "bad guys" and the Earthlings as the good. As his narrator says,

> Before we judge them too harshly, we must remember what ruthless and utter destruction our own species has brought to its fellow human beings as well as any animal species that got in its way. Can we complain if the Martians make war in the same spirit?

In other words, Wells seems to be saying, the strong have the right to vanquish the weak, and if the Martians have evolved into superior beings, they deserve to conquer us.

Wells's related belief that religion serves a false and ultimately useless function is clear when we consider the role of the priest in *The War of the Worlds*. As the narrator travels with the priest and hides with him from the Martians, it becomes obvious that the priest's faith in God offers him no hope or comfort in this situation. Instead, the priest swiftly sinks down to the level of an animal. He steals food from his companion and shows himself to be a weak, spineless man, frightened and foolish and no good to anyone.

The most significant glimpse into Wells's Darwinian morality comes in what can be seen in the narrator's meeting with the soldier, who explains his vision of what will occur in the future, once Earth is under control of the Martians. In this vision, most humans—particularly the soft, weak, "upper class"—will quickly accept their roles as the Martians' domestic animals and food source. But a small number of tough, unspoiled—that is, evolutionarily superior —humans will go "underground" and eventually learn enough Martian technology to turn it against the invaders. This small band of superior humans will evolve beyond the Martians, and will then be ready to be the masters once again.

Given Wells's faith in evolution, and his disdain for the weak and foolish of humanity, it surely must have given him some amusement to see thousands of people panicking over a radio show. He must have wondered how we Americans would have stood up to a *real* Martian invasion.